ELIZABETH BROMWELL

The Case of the

Chinese Leopard

KATHRYN RAAKER &
ROBERT M. TAGGART

Jan-Carol
Publishing, Inc

"every story needs a book"

Elizabeth Bromwell
The Adventures of an Expat Spy
The Case of the Chinese Leopard
Kathryn Raaker
Robert M. Taggart

Published December 2022
Little Creek Books
Imprint of Jan-Carol Publishing, Inc.
All rights reserved
Cover Design: Lynda Martini
Book Design: Tara Sizemore
Copyright © 2022 Kathryn Raaker and Robert M. Taggart

ISBN: 978-1-954978-71-3
Library of Congress Control Number: 2022950806

You may contact the publisher:
Jan-Carol Publishing, Inc.
PO Box 701
Johnson City, TN 37605
publisher@jancarolpublishing.com
www.jancarolpublishing.com

This book is dedicated to my Lord and Savior for the talents to create this adventure in writing. To my husband and partner, Bill, for all the help and support through the years. To our children and their families, and our extended families and friends worldwide. In loving memory of our parents. A BIG THANK YOU to all our readers for their feedback and encouragement to continue the series.

–K.R.

For Crystal (Double07), thank you for all of the adventures, love and devotion.

–R.T.

Author's Note

E lizabeth is a wife, mother, a soon-to-be-grandmother, and an undercover, decorated expat spy whose cover as a radio show host and encrypted messages have saved lives. She has risked her life in the field and lived secretly with the pain, keeping it hidden even from her husband, Carson, who is a world-renown golf course architect. In the latest adventure, everything Elizabeth knows will come into question: coming home, her health, her identity, dead friends, old romantic flames, and even her patriotism. I truly hope you enjoy this roller coaster ride.

My inspiration in writing this book was to imagine myself in Elizabeth's shoes and to create an adventure that galvanizes and excites the reader.

Foreword

By Fionne Foxxe Farraday
Author of *Kairn: Mates of the Alliance*

Elizabeth is a dynamic woman with an absolute gift for making people feel comfortable and engaged. She incorporates her sparkling personality and wit into the thought-provoking weft of this very enjoyable book. Get ready for a scintillating thrill ride that goes from zero to 100. Elizabeth's adventures promise a lot and deliver even more. Dear reader, the writers gleefully pull you in, immersing you in a complex world where first impressions can be deliciously, lethally deceiving. Exotic locales? Challenging plot twists that give a reader the very best kind of whiplash? Adventure with an underlying arc of international espionage? Survival of the free world hinging on a hairsbreadth decision? Plus the best part—trying to guess what's fiction and what's truth. Anchored by family, the close-knit relationships run wonderfully deep and provide a powerful bedrock to center the underlying message echoing through the book. What would you do for your family? Enjoy this intriguing peek into Elizabeth's life. I can't wait for her next riveting adventure.

CHAPTER 1

A beautiful orange glow stretched across dimming blue skies peppered with small popcorn clouds in 1993. Snow was not forecasted, but the icy winds forced the Assistant Director of the CIA, Charles Bridgewater, to put on his warm weather gear.

"Good night, sir," said Private First Class Nelson with a salute.

"As you were," Bridgewater responded and gave a quick salute.

He breathed the cold air into his lungs and exhaled a vapor cloud. His brutal day was just another part of his job function. Tomorrow would bring extended hours, phone calls, and team meetings with analysts. Today's events required a stiff drink to calm him down and warm his bones on such a cold day.

One hour ago, Bridgewater debriefed the president and the director of intelligence on their progress during a secure phone call. The president did not hesitate about what he expected from his deputy director of intelligence.

"I want results, Charles, and I know you are the man for the job," the commander in chief informed him. "Operation Angry Bird will flush out this SOB."

"Yes, we will succeed," he said confidently, and the call ended.

Now, he leaned back in his chair and rubbed his temples. He was sleep deprived after 24-hours of travel from Washington. He was here to investigate a threat to National Security. At this moment, the word of a leak was conjecture. But he knew there was a double agent, a mole. He looked at the classified files he had just read for the past few hours. He found it strange that highly trained field agents were ambushed, tortured, and killed. Those killed all seemed to play a part in the Tiananmen Square ordeal.

Bridgewater reminisced for a moment. As a young Army Captain working in the Pentagon, the president's top brass recognized his accomplishments in analyzing, decoding, translating, and advising on intelligence matters in 1984. In the background, the company also took notice of his skills and approached Bridgewater. Once his time with the Army ended, he was recruited into the CIA.

The following year, he enhanced his skills at the farm. The mind-numbing and grueling training set him up to be an operative.

Black folder in hand, he opened it to find his first assignment would be served in the eastern block for two years. He was promoted quickly and served as an operative in South America for a year.

In 1989, Bridgewater and other CIA officers were assigned to secure and rescue democratic protestors from the Chinese communist army during the Tiananmen Square massacre on June 4.

The operation involved the British Intelligence Agency MI5 working with the CIA and other politicians, celebrities, and even local gang members to get people to safety. For weeks, the Chinese government sent out its troops looking for 40 people identified as the ringleaders to capture and torture them.

Yellowbird, he thought. This was the code name of the operation that set many Chinese protesting citizens free from tyranny and gave them a new life. He earned his code name "Wild Turkey" with the unorthodox and efficient way he saved lives.

Bridgewater led the covert mission and met a Chinese national who captured his heart. She was in trouble in Tiananmen Square. Accosted by several soldiers, she put up a fantastic battle by knocking out three of the men. The rest ran when Bridgewater and a few other CIA agents ran at them with guns drawn and chased the soldiers away.

Meili Zhen picked herself up off the ground and looked at Bridgewater. She was 5'9" with long legs, short black hair, and complementing amber eyes, and she spoke fluent English and several other languages. Zhen studied abroad in France and then began a career as a nurse and part-time demonstrator for democracy. During the protests, she dressed as the Goddess of Democracy.

Zhen accompanied Bridgewater back to Washington only to fall in love with him. They would marry and have two children: a son and a daughter. Bridgewater felt some regret missing family dinners and events when he traveled.

That year, he was promoted to run the Hong Kong division as the station chief. Most nights, he worked late and would unwind at a local dive bar called The Last Resort. The Chinese government was constantly monitoring Americans. They believed they were spies. His cover was impeccable, and to the local patrons, he was known as a chain-smoking industrial traveling salesman that liked to drink and tell stories.

He could not remember when his last visit was to The Last Resort. He wondered if his favorite bartender was still employed.

A cold gust of wind kicked up leaves and sent a chill through him. He buttoned his coat, wrapped his scarf around his neck, and began to think about a classified cable he read before leaving the office. He was so immersed in thought that he caught a raised stone in the street with his dress shoe and nearly fell over.

For shit's sake, be careful where you're walking, he scolded himself. He was 6'2" and in incredible athletic shape for being a desk captain. He pushed himself to be the best and had great instincts.

And at that moment, he felt as if he was being tailed. He crossed Pottinger street to look in the window of a bakery, but the sun was setting, and shadows made it hard to see any reflections. However, no people were moving from what he saw behind him.

The last resort had a black door with a curtain. He pushed it aside; neon lights lit up the room, arcade games summoned players, and pool sharks circled the tables looking for their next victim.

As he sat down at the bar, Fuji Lee greeted him. She nearly screamed, saying his name. She noticed that age had not changed his handsome features. Bridgewater's brown eyes, high cheekbones, square jaw, and trimmed beard attracted most women who knew him.

She remembered how Bridgewater saved her and others during the 1989 chaos. Fuji was held at gunpoint by a Chinese soldier in a small alley. Bridgewater heard her scream while walking to meet his team. He peeked around the corner of the alley. Fuji's eyes met his, and he put his finger up to his mouth motioning her to be quiet. His demeanor was cool and calm in reacting to the situation. Seeing a half-filled beer bottle in the street, he poured the beer over his head and ran his fingers in his hair. Bridgewater looked like a bum to the irate soldier and drunkenly stumbled up to him. The soldier yelled at him to move, but he stumbled and punched him when he was close enough, knocking the young soldier unconscious. She moved away to a town in eastern China until the political unrest settled down.

"Where have you been?" she said, walking around the bar to hug him.

"Around this great world!" he replied.

"Missed you, Mr. B," she whispered in his ear.

"Hey, Mr. B, same poison as always?" she smiled widely and gave a little giggle.

"A double bourbon," he began and frowned.

"On the rocks," she completed the sentence.

"Bad day, Mr. B?" she asked.

"Uh-huh. You could say that."

She poured the drink, added a little umbrella, and laughed.

"I hope sales get better, Mr. B," she said and then went to serve another customer.

Under his leadership in Hong Kong, there were limited casualties during covert operations. He was here to investigate seven officers' deaths in the past six months. The autopsy photos were gruesome. The killer always cut his symbol on some part of their body. It looked like the sign of Libra—a line with an arc and another line underneath.

What the hell is going on, Wilkerson? Bridgewater thought. After being promoted as deputy director of the CIA, his assistant, Ken Wilkerson, was encouraged to take his place as the station chief.

Good officers were now dead, and Bridgewater wanted answers. Wilkerson was responsible for Hong Kong and keeping the secret service and U.S. secret information from falling into enemy hands. There would be a scathing conversation when the two were together for a debriefing.

"Hey, Fuji," Bridgewater said as he tapped the edge of his glass.

"For sure," she said before pouring more bourbon.

He sat for a while and bemoaned a tragic thought that any operation officer could be a traitor. *Could one of his former officers honestly have planned the bombing that killed two agents in the World Trade Center?* His mind veered to Elizabeth Bromwell on an undercover assignment in New York for a radio convention. He wanted to wish her success, but he never got a chance to call her.

"Fuji, got a Marlboro and a light?"

She motioned for him to step over to the side of the bar where the patrons could not see. She kissed him on the lips, then put the Marlboro in his mouth and lit it for him. She pushed him out a side door into an alley, kissing him again in the dark.

"We can't do this anymore, Fuji. I'm married with children," he said in a parental tone.

She kissed him again and turned her back as if nothing had happened.

"I have to watch these freeloaders. Need to keep this job," she said.

An overhead light dimly lit the dark alley. Bridgewater inhaled the cigarette smoke into his lungs and puffed a circle out of his mouth.

"They say that shit will kill you," the voice said.

Bridgewater thought he could see a figure but didn't know where the voice was coming from, and then unexplainably, a puff of smoke engulfed him. He gagged and began coughing. Blood started dripping from his nose, and his body hurt. He fell to his knees, and his cigarette dropped to the ground.

The footsteps came from behind him. He leaned forward and realized he could not breathe. He wiped his eyes, and they were bleeding.

"The American Government abandoned me when I was captured and tortured. And, now, they will feel the wrath of my team," the assassin said. "Tell me where the Harbinger file is, and your death won't be in vain."

Bridgewater tried to speak but coughed on his blood. His eyes burned, bulged, and he could feel himself blacking out. He let out a gurgled response.

"Go to hell," Bridgewater said, choking.

He wished he had not come to his old hangout, not given his last kiss ever to Fuji. Bridgewater's final thoughts settled on his wife and children.

"Please forgive me?" Bridgewater whispered. Then, his body went limp and crumpled to the ground.

"No, idiot, I won't forgive you! I am the beast that will kill every agent until I complete my mission!" he yelled.

"I am the leopard that will rip and shred away at America's freedom," the masked attacker exclaimed.

The assassin pulled out a lighter, heated a logo on a ring he was wearing on his forefinger, and seared the symbol on Bridgewater's forehead.

"Your country has no idea what is coming," he said to the corpse before disappearing into the darkness.

Fuji came back out from the bar to apologize. Her high-pitched scream alerted everyone in the bar. Patrons found Fuji wailing over Bridgewater's dead body lying on the ground.

CHAPTER 2

The yellow and black taxi pulled to the curb and stopped right in front of one of the most revered delicatessens in Manhattan. This New York cabbie, known as Cassali, had earned a reputation for entertaining visitors. He stretched his meter by "giving 'em the tour." The longer the ride, the more money that padded his wallet. Some fares just thought the driver eccentric.

Cassali wasn't the usual New York cabbie. He wore a top hat, which went surprisingly well with his tuxedo T-shirt, black jean shorts, and black Army boots to finish the ensemble. He was of Indian descent, but you would never know it by how he spoke.

He glanced in his rear-view mirror at the two passengers in his back seat. Jacob and Janet Jordon peered out the window at the historic establishment located in the same place on 7th avenue since 1937.

"Here you go! Welcome to Carnegie Deli," Cassali shouted to Jacob and Janet in his thick New York accent. "Nice choice, you two. They do an a-mazing cream cheese bagel, soup, a great pastrami sandwich, yadda, yada, yadda..."

Jacob paid the driver $20, even though the meter registered a $17.32 charge. "Keep the change, and thanks for the show and getting us here without issue," Jacob said. He knew the driver had delayed their arrival by cutting through the theatre district of Manhattan. This was Janet's first trip to New York, so he didn't mention it.

Opening the taxi door, Jacob was greeted by a gust of cold wind and snow flurries that chilled him to the bone, even though he was bundled up in a North Face winter jacket and a colorful scarf around his neck.

February never felt so cold, he thought. He held out his hand for his very pregnant wife, who slowly scooted along with the leather-stitched seat.

"Thanks, babe. You're such a gentleman," she said, stepping onto the snowy curb in front of the red and yellow neon sign reading *Carnegie Delicatessen Restaurant*.

As they entered the six-decade old Jewish deli, Jacob breathed in the aroma of the fresh-baked rye bread and olive oil, and in his mind, he swore he could almost taste the pastrami. The crowded restaurant was loud with conversation. The café was quaint and popular. Signed photographs of celebrities lined the walls.

Good man, Jacob thought. This seemed to be a good choice since his wife was craving sweets and anything salty. He figured she might even order a pickle with her lunch. The tables were filled with patrons talking, with some watching the New York Rangers game against the Calgary Flames. They were tied 4–4 with less than 30 seconds left in overtime.

Ka-BOOM! The sound turned heads in the restaurant and even knocked a plate off one of the tables nearby. Jacob and Janet were about to kiss. Jacob had closed his eyes while Janet was looking out the plate glass window to the outside of the restaurant, where a crowd of 30 people were gathering and pointing.

"Jacob, what the hell was that?" Janet asked with a panic-stricken look. Jacob opened his eyes to see the horror on her face.

"I am sure it's nothing, babe, maybe the backfire of a truck?" Jacob said, trying to calm his wife.

"Jacob Bromwell! Don't patronize me," she said as she turned and headed to the door.

The crowd was pointing at a large plume of black smoke in the distance coming from one of the giant skyscrapers.

A truck slammed on its brakes in front of the restaurant and slid into the back of an empty taxi, demolishing the trunk.

A cantankerous Jewish man emerged from the taxi waving his hands and shouting at the truck driver over his radio, ironically blasting the Bon Jovi song, "Wild in the Streets."

Half the crowd was fixated on the accident. A large black man jumped out of the driver's seat of the truck and began to poke his finger in the chest of the taxi driver.

The other half was trying to figure out what had happened in the city.

A man with a southern accent quipped, "I think there is smoke coming from the Empire State Building."

Janet corrected him immediately. "Huh? I'm sorry, sir, but the Empire State Building is three miles north."

He was a small man dressed in jeans, boots, a cowboy hat, and a denim jacket with a wool collar. The cowboy had a long red mustache to match his long red hair. He laughed at Janet with the amazement that someone would correct him. He touched his brim.

"I sure am sorry about that, ma'am. I am just a good ol' country boy traveling this state," the cowboy said with a deep voice and a blushing red face. He reminded her of Yosemite Sam.

"Sorry, I don't know why I just blurted that out," she said.

Over the fighting and the conversation around them, Jacob heard the music change to a news report. A three-tone sound came across the radio. "This is a special report from WPIX," a gravelly voice announced. "There has been an explosion at the World Trade Center, and many are believed to be trapped in the building. Again, a large blast has rocked the World Trade Center."

"Babe, we need to find a pay phone right away!" Jacob shouted.

"What? Why do we need...?" Jacob pulled her close.

"Listen, babe. My mom is attending the National Radio Broadcast convention luncheon today at the World Trade Center, which is now on fire! I need to call her on her Nokia, but we need to find a payphone."

Large snow flurries fell, sticking to the sidewalk. Two blocks from the café, they squeezed into a small phone booth, relieved to get out of the elements.

He dropped two quarters into the pay slot, dialed, and listened. After several rings and no answer, he hung up the phone. He called again.

"Nothing," he said to his wife. He called again, this time leaving a message.

"Mom, if you get this voicemail anytime soon, please let me know you are okay by paging me back," he said, shaky, and hung up the phone.

"Jacob, call your dad to see if he knows what is happening," Janet said, putting her arm around him.

"It's late in Singapore right now, but he needs to know what is happening," Jacob admitted. "Operator, I like to make a collect call please to the following number..."

CHAPTER 3

"Hell-o?" Carson Jordon answered in a slumbered voice.

"Dad, it's Jacob. Can you hear me?"

"What time is it?" he asked.

"Early! But have you heard what happened here?"

"Son, at 3:10 a.m., you want to tell me about your trip to New York?"

"No, Dad, it's about Mom. She is at a meeting at the Towers, and something terrible has happened."

"What are you talking about, Jacob?" his dad asked as sirens blared in the background.

"There was a large explosion at the World Trade Center, and Mom is supposed to be at lunch there today, Dad."

Jacob heard a loud thud.

"Dad...Dad...Hey, Pops." Jacob thought the call had disconnected. Then he heard something in the background.

Jacob felt a tug on his arm as his wife pressed behind him in the telephone booth. It was frigid, but she was keeping him warm.

"What happened to your dad?" she inquired.

Carson turned the television on to the Sky World News. The New York World Trade Center was the headline story. The red banner at the top screen read, *Special News Report: Hundreds Injured at World Trade Center Bombing.*

The newscast flashed a video clip from CNN, a New York news affiliate, of a large smoke plume coming from the garage of the building. Carson also noticed a number flashing on the screen for information on family members: 1-800-222-1333. Carson grabbed the phone he had just dropped seconds ago and said the number aloud as he wrote it down.

Janet snatched the phone and pulled Jacob close to her so she could hear as well. "What did you just say, Dad?" Jacob asked.

"Jacob, dial this number..."

Carson hung up the phone and started making plans to get on the earliest flight to New York.

CHAPTER 4

Elizabeth grabbed her concealment purse and followed a group of 12 people from her table to the emergency exit. The NRBA Vice President Justin Snow had reached 911 and was told to evacuate all members from the 107th floor to the 110th floor. This was considered not to be accessible to the public. Still, the fire department would attempt to land near the radio antennae on the roof and evacuate as many as possible. The heavy snow would also present issues.

"Let's agree to hold on to the railings, everyone," Elizabeth suggested, and everyone seemed to shake their heads in agreement.

Elizabeth began climbing the stairs, following as if she were part of a herd of cattle. The billowing smoke smelled like burnt barbecue, and she didn't want to be a participant in this cook-off. An older woman in front slipped and fell, and she grabbed her hand.

"Are you okay?" she asked.

"Yes. Thank you, darling."

"Okay, hold on to that railing and keep climbing."

She felt for the next step, and as quickly as she placed her foot on the step, a large hand grabbed her shoulder and pulled her backward. She was thrown into a wall and became winded. She could no longer see the group marching up the stairs. The black smoke only revealed a shadow of her purse a few feet away and the large shadow approaching. Slowly, she slid into a crouching position against the wall.

"What, why did you...?" she quipped before the massive figure kicked her so hard she screamed and could not breathe. Her arm felt like it was on fire as she tried to protect herself from the blow.

The dark figure stood over her. She winced and looked up to see him bending over in her face. He wore a bandana over his mouth and held a .38 in his hand that had a weird brand tattooed on it.

"Where is the Harbinger file?" he asked in a muffled voice.

Dazed, confused, and short of breath, she launched herself from the crouching position and sent her knee into his groin. He doubled over, moaned in pain, and cursed at Elizabeth. He dropped a handgun that bounced off the cement and landed at her attacker's feet. Elizabeth launched forward and scrambled to pick up the firearm with her right hand, but this hurt terribly. She fumbled with the gun in her left hand and pulled the trigger accidentally, shooting her attacker in the shoulder.

"Shit!" she yelled and stumbled, getting up to run away into the pitch-black fog.

"Aah, you dumb, dumb bitch!" the large man exclaimed, grabbing his shoulder in pain. As Elizabeth tried to escape him, the man threw out his leg and knocked her off balance. Elizabeth wobbled, the gun fell out of her hand, and she rolled down the stairs, reaching out for the handrails before the impact of the next floor took her breath away again. She looked up, and everything turned black.

CHAPTER 5

Nearly 48 hours had passed, and Ken Wilkerson found himself on a CIA Boeing 737 transporting the body of his former deputy director. He was numb, tired, and irritated with all the phone calls he received from CIA Crime Division, the press secretary, and other high-ranking officials. Additionally, 23 hours in-flight meant less sleep and cramped muscles. At 33, he was one of the youngest Station Chief assigned to the Asian Division.

Bridgewater would be buried in Arlington, Virginia, with other American soldiers who gave their lives for the country. He served with Charlie in the Army Delta Force. Both were involved in Operation Urgent Fury with the takeover of Grenada. On October 24, the Delta unit reconnoitered Pointe Salines to the day before the attack.

The reconnaissance was invaluable as the enemy was heavily armed with a stockpile of weapons, including Kalashnikov AKSU-74 submachine guns. While they did not lose any men in their unit, several soldiers in other units were wounded or lost their lives. They faced stiff opposition. Wilkerson was injured on the north end of Pointe Saliens and carried out of the firefight by Charlie.

Charlie was influential in recruiting Wilkerson into the directorate of operations of the CIA in 1987. However, their relationship was strained after Operation Red Bird he planned went awry. Wilkerson would take a leave of absence after losing his soulmate and having his reputation tarnished.

Wilkerson pondered for a moment and became enraged thinking about having to bury Bridgewater. He slammed his hand into the empty seat in front of him.

For the past few years, his time spent as the head of Hong Kong had gone to his satisfaction. Then the killings began, and a deadly toxin killed several operation officers and an analyst. The company (known as the CIA) had frowned upon his leadership.

"Sir, would you like some coffee?" the attending Sergeant asked.

"Yes, thank you. Do you have Bailey's to go along with it?" Wilkerson smiled.

"No, sir," she said and poured the coffee into a large cup. "But maybe I have something better."

When she returned, she handed him a giant cookie. He took a sip of the black coffee and then a bite of the chocolate chip cookie.

"Sweet," he said and smiled.

This day would be long and arduous, with meetings scheduled at Langley with not only CIA officials, but also the Joint Intelligence Committee and the Secretary of Defense.

"Want some company, sir?" asked Max Frost, a senior counterintelligence officer.

"Sure, sit down, Max," Wilkerson said, taking a long sip of his coffee. "Are you attending at Arlington?"

"Yes and no," Frost said.

"Sounds complicated," Wilkerson said.

"It is. I am working detail," Frost said. "Wild Turkey was a good man."

Wilkerson just nodded his head. He wondered why Frost said yes and no.

"I am sorry to hear about Hong Kong," Frost said. He knew he could not say anything further, seeing as he was involved in the investigation of the murdered agents.

Frost was a reliable operations officer stationed all over Asia, Russia, and part of Latin America. He thoroughly analyzed and investigated which agent was playing in the U.S. sandbox and those who played in China. In his estimation, less than 20 CIA operatives played both sides of the fence.

"Thank you," Wilkerson said. "Truthfully, I am not looking forward to the next few days."

At that moment, they were interrupted by the attending sergeant.

"Sirs, we are about to descend into San Francisco Airport, and I will need to ask you both to prepare for our arrival," she said.

They hit an air pocket, and the plane dropped, and she caught herself from falling.

"This occasionally happens when we get close to the ground," she said, exasperated and embarrassed.

"What is the stopover time to refuel?" Wilkerson asked.

"I believe we will stop for the next 45 minutes," she answered. "It should give you some time to stretch your legs and make secure calls."

The sergeant grabbed the coffee cup, napkin, and plastic wrap of the cookie and headed to the back of the plane to clean up and get to her seat. Frost turned to watch her. He admired her tight ass and long legs in her blue Air Force Dress.

Frost's attention was diverted back to the sound of Wilkerson's pager. Wilkerson picked up the pager to look at the screen and studied it for a moment before putting it down. Frost had caught a glimpse of the text on the screen, which looked like an international number.

"Nice seeing you, Ken," Frost said as he stood up and headed back to his seat.

"Uh-huh. You too," Wilkerson said with a wave.

Wilkerson took his pager off the fold-out table and switched it to vibrate. He placed it on the seat vacated by Frost. He wondered if he was prepared to meet with the CIA Director Sean Cookson.

He contemplated the type of internal and external investigation the CIA had planned. As the diplomat, the death of his operation officers presented a tumultuous situation. Thankfully, he knew the proper heads of state and planned these scenarios effectively. He would have some answers soon. The attendant was back in front of him.

"Sir. Buckle your seat belt, please," the sergeant said. She was doing her last check before landing.

"Uh-huh, will do," Wilkerson said. His pager buzzed and nearly fell to the floor. He grabbed the pager and read the text on the screen. *The cat is out of the bag.*

CHAPTER 6

The screams echoed, and Elizabeth couldn't figure out exactly where they were coming from. She blacked out at some point, and when she awoke, her body shivered in the cold catacomb of the stairwell.

Her body curled tightly around the metal railing, and her heart raced with anxiety. She tried to pull herself up to walk but felt too weak and crumbled to the floor. She felt woozy and began to cough. She thought someone was standing over her, but her eyes burned, and her head ached.

The dark black smoke smelled like rotten eggs, but her lungs burned with each labored breath. In the distance was an image coming closer to her, and the sound of mechanical breathing reminded her of Darth Vader in *Star Wars*.

The figure in a black helmet took off his gloves and grabbed her wrist with two fingers.

"She's alive," the large, burly man said. He momentarily pulled off his helmet and oxygen mask and put it on her face. She breathed in fresh air only to cough in the fireman's mask. The air was pure and, for a moment, reminded her of rising from the ocean's depths to the surface and grabbing the first breath.

Her eyes burned, yet she was happy someone had found her. She could barely make out the fireman, who looked older and had a commanding voice.

"If you can hear me, just raise your hand." Elizabeth complied by slowly raising her hand, but the weight of her Gucci purse twisting around her arm made it difficult. "Okay, we will roll you on your back and have you lay flat, so we can help you out of here."

The smoke billowing up the staircase was hot and black. A younger fireman assisting him was talking on his radio.

"Cap, they will meet us on the roof in five. I got a collar ready to go," the younger fireman said.

Elizabeth's head ached as they immobilized her neck.

"Carson?" she mumbled in a shallow breath to the younger firefighter. She could hardly breathe. Her ribs felt like someone had stabbed her.

"No, but I wish I was Johnny," he said, joking. As he placed an oxygen mask on Elizabeth, she began screaming and flailing. "Where is Carson, my husband!"

"Whoa, darling, settle down. We are here to help," the older firefighter commanded.

"Breathe, Elizabeth," she commanded herself.

She let out a grunt and opened her eyes. The two firemen carried her on a backboard up the final steps to the exit door. The door flung open with swirling freezing snow and cold gusts from an awaiting emergency helicopter.

Two paramedics ran up to the firefighters with a rolling gurney.

"She is a live wire," he warned one of the paramedics. They loaded her onto the rolling gurney from the backboard and headed to the medevac helicopter.

"Ma'am, keep your eyes focused on me," one of the paramedics said as the firefighters lifted her into the chopper. "You need to calm down. Slow your breathing. Your blood pressure is very high."

Elizabeth thought she heard what he said over the rotating blades but felt dazed and confused.

"You're quite safe. Try to relax. We are taking you to the hospital. You took a nice fall. Firemen said they found you tied to the guard rail like a pretzel."

Elizabeth tried to remove the oxygen mask from her face so she could speak.

"Don't try to move your arms. We had to put one in a sling, and I just put an IV drip in the other. There is also a dressing on a nasty cut on your head, and you may have a concussion," he said as the helicopter lifted off the pad.

"Thank God for the NYFD," she tried to say, but nothing came out. Her mouth was dry, and her tongue felt sore as if she bit it.

She began to panic and breath quickly.

Why can't I seem to focus? Her thoughts raced to the building shaking and then her fall. *Everything is going black,* and she was out. A cold sensation raced up her arm. "Ma'am, don't fall asleep," said a medical technician encouraging her to stay awake on the short flight to the hospital. "My name is Jake. What's your name?"

"Eli-z-abeth," her voice cracked as she tried to tell Jake, "That's my son's name."

He checked her vitals and shined a penlight in her pupil to see how it would react. He kept speaking to her until they landed at the hospital.

A nurse met the paramedics wheeling her on the stretcher at the flight pad. Wheeling her into the emergency room, the nurse asked her name.

"I am Elizabeth," she blurted. "No, that's not right. It's Elizabeth Jordan."

The nurse laughed. "That's alright, sugar. It's whatever name you want me to use." Then, she proceeded to gather as much medical and family history from Elizabeth.

"Can I get some water?" Elizabeth asked.

"Sorry, Mrs. Jordan, I'm Doctor Chad Michael, and we need to assess all your injuries before you can have anything to drink, just in case we need to give you an anesthetic," he said with a Cheshire grin. "Perhaps some ice after we know more."

After a thorough examination, which included X-rays, an MRI, and blood tests, Elizabeth was still desperate for some water. And since it seemed like hours had passed, she thought Dr. Michael had lied to her.

"I need something to drink. I have cotton mouth," she told the attending nurse.

"I bet with all the black smoke and other chemicals you breathed in," Dr. Michael explained as he walked into the room with a large cup of water. "Slow sips, okay?"

She tried not to take a large gulp, but her palette demanded differently. "Sorry," she answered in a child-like voice with wide eyes and shrugged shoulders.

"It's okay. Many patients do the same thing you just did. Don't get sick on me, okay?" the doctor requested with a large, white-toothed smile.

Elizabeth felt woozy but ingratiated knowing she had a doctor who cared. And, to go along with his impeccable oral hygiene was his chiseled face. He had high cheekbones and a cleft in his chin. If she didn't know any better, she would have sworn he doubled as an actor in one soap opera.

Holding her medical chart in his hand, he began reading the breakdown of her injuries. "You have a grade 2 concussion, a stress fracture in your left hand, broken ribs, and multiple bruising. No major organs were injured, but you will be here for at least a week or two before release."

"But I have a radio show..." she responded.

"No, I am afraid your audience will have to listen to your other recorded shows for a while. Also, Dr. Amarillo Ellis will be stopping by in a few minutes to test your blood gases and breathing," he explained. "She is our local pulmonologist. She will run some tests for any smoke inhalation damage. We will move you to a private room where your family can visit."

Once her hand was bandaged with a metal plate to protect it, she was settled in a private room. The nurse came in to fill her water and give her medication to ease her pain.

"Okay, sugar, I am going to change out your saline. My name is nurse Cynthia Laveaux, and if you haven't noticed, I'm from New Orleans," she laughed aloud. "You can call me Cynthia if you like.

Dr. Michael has prescribed some sedatives to help you relax from any kind of anxiety."

"I prefer not to take sedatives," said Elizabeth.

"Oh, but..." the nurse started to say.

"No buts," Elizabeth responded quickly, "I do not want sedatives."

"Okay, Cherie, you're the boss of yourself," she chuckled.

"I'm sorry, I just prefer to be conscious after being unconscious and unsure of what happened," Elizabeth apologized. "How many others?"

"Others?" Nurse Laveaux asked with a perplexed look on her face.

"How many people made it out of the World Trade Center bombing?"

"Let's just say this. You are quite fortunate, Cherie. We're short staffed after hundreds were injured. Some with crushed limbs. Some who passed on to the upper floors."

Elizabeth could only close her eyes. A tear rolled down her cheek, and she wished Carson was here.

"Carson!" she exclaimed.

"Settle down there, Cherie, you nearly ripped out your IV sitting up so fast," the nurse exclaimed.

"Sorry, it's my husband, nurse. He is in Singapore, and I don't even know if he knows what happened yet," Elizabeth lamented.

"I am sure he does. It's the top story on every local and international radio and television channel," Laveaux said. "Do you have any other family members?"

"Yep, Jacob..." she said in deep thought.

"Jacob, huh?" Laveaux said.

"He's my son!" Elizabeth grinned. "He is a wonderful man and is married with a newborn on the way."

"Well, Grandma, better get you well soon." Laveaux chuckled.

CHAPTER 7

Jacob arrived at the hospital with Janet squeezing his hand. Dr. Michael met with him before going in to see his mom.

"Your mom has some minor injuries and will require some time to rest. But she needs to listen to her doctor. She is refusing the sedatives that will help her relax," he said.

Jacob chuckled as he turned to look through his mother's hospital room window.

"That doesn't surprise me. Mom likes to be in control and know what's going on, and she never stops. We call her the Energizer Bunny."

The doctor smiled and nodded, "A little persuasion might be futile, but it would keep her stable and help her get some needed rest."

Janet couldn't hold back a snorting laugh. "Sorry. But you don't know his mother."

"In any case, it would certainly help with her pain," he explained.

They all walked into Elizabeth's room.

"Jacob and Janet," she said with a hoarse voice. "I was so scared I would never see my grandbaby being born." Tears rolled down her face.

The doctor motioned the nurse to leave the room.

"Okay, Elizabeth, I'll leave you to talk with your son and daughter-in-law now and check back on you tonight."

"Thank you, doctor," they all said in unison.

"How did you two find me?" Elizabeth asked, astonished.

Jacob explained that he had tried to call his mother on her cell phone. When there was no reply, he left a message for her to message him on his pager.

"I fell and have no idea where my cell phone is now," she said.

"Well, when I didn't hear from you, I called Dad, and he gave me an emergency number to call. I kept getting a busy signal, but finally an operator answered. However, they couldn't tell me exactly where you were. Frustrated, I started yelling and sobbing," he said sadly. "If it weren't for my patient wife making the calls to the local hospitals, we'd be stuck in the cold."

Jacob gave his mom a gentle hug and said, "So, expat, you look battle worn. How are you feeling?" Suddenly, his wife punched his arm and scolded him. "Jacob!"

"It's okay, honey. We know he can be a real jerk at times. I know I raised him to be better than that," she laughed and winced in pain, remembering she had broken ribs.

Jacob felt horrible. "You okay, Mom?"

"No. I have two fractured ribs, a stress fracture in my hand, and a concussion, but I doubt that will stop me."

Elizabeth was so pleased to see her son but struggled to understand what had happened. It frustrated her that she could not remember many details of the incident.

"I'm Okay," she told him, "Now, tell me what you will name our grandbaby, Janet. How are you feeling?"

"Well, Mom, Jacob and I decided on Lizzie Ann," Janet said with a glowing face.

Cynthia came back into the room. Just then, the phone next to her bed started to ring. "Cherie, you might want to take that call."

The phone was positioned to her left, but Jacob picked up the receiver and handed it to her.

"Hello?" Elizabeth said. It was Carson calling from the airport. "My love, I am okay. No, you don't have to come to New York."

Carson explained his flight was boarding, and nothing could stop him from being there for her.

"I love you so much," she told him and then handed the phone to Jacob, who wanted to speak to his dad but heard a dial tone instead.

"Jacob, he had to catch his flight," she explained.

They visited for an hour before Jacob decided to take his wife back to their hotel to eat and rest. He convinced his mom to take the sedatives that the doctor prescribed. Elizabeth felt drowsy and closed her eyes when Cynthia popped back into the room to check her vitals.

"Cherie, you need rest, but your aunt Estelle is here. What a lovely woman."

"Really?" Elizabeth's adrenaline kicked in, and she immediately sat up.

"Keep it short. You must rest now after what you have been through today," Cynthia said.

Estelle entered the room with a large basket of fruit, flowers, clean clothes, and a toiletry bag.

"How are you, my love?" she asked. Estelle was dressed in a blue, pin-striped mid-knee dress that looked like an Armani suit with lace lapels and six gold buttons. She wore blue Bandolino Lantana dress shoes to match.

Elizabeth began to cry again. "How did you know, auntie?"

"You know I have a network of people," she said jokingly. "No, dear, Jacob called me, of course, and let me know what was happening."

"How did you get here so fast?" Elizabeth asked as she looked at the clock on the wall. The clock read 8:00 p.m.

"I was traveling in Washington D.C., and a dignitary friend put me on his private jet once I heard what happened," she explained. "I gathered your belongings at your hotel and settled your account before visiting the hospital."

Typical of Estelle, thought Elizabeth. *She always knows what to do.*

Elizabeth started to ask questions regarding the other people trapped at the convention. "Wait a minute, Elizabeth," said Estelle, "First things first. Tell me, how are you feeling?"

"I am in terrible pain," she said as she began coughing.

"Elizabeth, please slow down. I know you want answers, but you need to relax and breathe." She gave Elizabeth her water. Estelle knew that smoke inhalation and her broken ribs would make breathing painful.

Tears formed in Elizabeth's eyes. "I can't get rid of the smell of smoke," she sobbed. "I've got a horrible taste in my mouth, and my throat feels like it's full of broken glass. When I cough, my chest feels as though it will burst."

Estelle put her arm gently around Elizabeth's shoulders and said, "Take your time, sweetheart. There's no rush. I'm not going anywhere."

Estelle's reassuring words and gentle touch calmed her a little, so Elizabeth continued, "I hurt all over, so whatever you do, don't make me laugh!"

"That's my girl," smiled Estelle. "Now, what do you want to know about what happened today?"

Estelle answered her questions and explained that it was a terrorist bomb that had exploded in the garages beneath the building. All the power in the building went out, and people on the upper floors were evacuated by helicopter.

Elizabeth started shaking and struggled to speak coherently. Estelle pressed the call button for assistance.

Cynthia leaned into the room. "What's going on, my Cherie?"

"I think it's time for me to find a cup of tea," Estelle said.

"No, if you please, I don't want to interrupt your time with your niece," Cynthia pleaded.

"No, it's fine," Estelle replied, so Cynthia began checking Elizabeth's temperature and blood pressure, and replacing her saline IV.

"Dr. Michael will be here shortly." At that moment, the doctor came in and studied Elizabeth's chart.

"Cynthia, please go check Mrs. Stravinsky in room 319," he said harshly before turning his attention to Estelle. "Well, hello. I am Dr. Michael. Glad to meet your acquaintance," he said, holding out his hand.

"The pleasure is mine. I appreciate your care for my niece, doctor," Estelle said, studying the young physician.

"Elizabeth, it is common for patients to feel shocked after a traumatic event. I will recommend a few pain killers and add a sedative to your IV drip to provide some pain relief and some sleep."

Elizabeth thought about objecting, but she knew it might be one battle she would not win. Everyone kept talking about sleep, and she needed it badly.

"Might I have your ear for a moment, Dr. Michael?" Estelle asked. They walked out of the room. "I don't want you pumping her full of narcotics. Is that clear?"

"I assure you she will be treated with the utmost..."

"You'd better, because I know several physicians and don't want to have to bring one at a special request of the hospital. I will be staying here and will be watching you."

"I understand," he said sheepishly.

"And, if you please, I could use a cup of tea," Estelle requested.

The doctor entered the room with Estelle. His face was flush, and Elizabeth knew Estelle had a moment with her doctor. He pushed the attendant button, and nurse Laveaux entered the room.

"Yes, doctor, how may I help?" nurse Laveaux asked.

"Nurse, could you please bring a mild sedative for Mrs. Bromwell so she can get some rest?" he requested and provided the dosage needed. "And, could you please bring her aunt some hot tea and an extra blanket...please?"

Nurse Cynthia Laveaux had never seen this side of the doctor before. *Did he say please more than once?* she thought.

As the nurse left the room, Elizabeth looked over at her aunt, who winked back.

"Mrs. Bromwell, I will see you to run more tests in the morning. Please have a pleasant night," the doctor said awkwardly.

Estelle and Elizabeth laughed.

"Damn..." Elizabeth said, holding her side in terrible pain. "I told you not to make me laugh, Aunt Estelle!"

Nurse Laveaux entered the room with the hot tea.

"Here you go, Cherie," handing Estelle the large cup of tea.

Seeing her niece trembling, she stood up and held the cup for Elizabeth so she could slowly sip the tea. The nurse then added the prescribed sedative to the IV drip.

After nearly 15 minutes of catching up on the latest news on new expat assignments, her aunt Estelle fell asleep.

Elizabeth started to replay the scary moments of the day. She remembered she was guided to her seat and looked out over the bustling street scene just 107 floors below the Windows of the World restaurant while thoroughly enjoying her dining experience in the excellent establishment. Her phone rang several times, but she did not pick up in time.

One of the men seated next to her asked her about her radio show. She wanted to desperately tell him she was an expat, working with the CIA to send messages to save lives.

Suddenly, the lights began flickering and went out. The building was swaying. It felt like an earthquake. Dishes fell from the table and broke. Pandemonium broke out, and she heard the guest speaker yell, "It will be fine! Please calm yourselves!"

Snow's phone rang, and his face turned ghost white as he closed his handheld phone. He informed everyone there had been an explosion in the basement garages, so all electricity was off, which meant the elevators were not operating. Black smoke began to pour through the air conditioning vents.

Security told everyone to stay put and that everything would be fine. As most diners tried to remain calm and wait for further information and instructions, others began to panic.

A couple of women screamed, and another one fainted. A man who used a wheelchair was bombastic, yelling loudly and demanding to know how he could get out without the elevator.

As the tension in the room began to rise, so did the smoke, growing from under the doors and seemingly through the floor. Elizabeth knew she couldn't just sit there and wait for instructions. She instructed everyone at her table to wet their napkins with water to cover their mouth and nose. Other patrons at other tables saw this and quickly followed suit.

She remembered being evacuated to the top floor. As a healthy, vibrant woman, Elizabeth found herself in one of the last groups directed to the stairs, routed to the roof. Emergency helicopters would airlift them to safety.

Elizabeth remembered falling. Something was nagging at her. And then she remembered hitting a wall, and a man was just standing there looking at her. It was faint but discernible. Frustrated, she opened her eyes and was back in her bed looking at Estelle slumped in a chair sleeping, breathing heavily.

She closed her eyes once again and began to think of Carson.

"Carson," she whispered...and faded off.

CHAPTER 8

Fire engines and whining police sirens could be heard all over New York City in response to a bombing at the World Trade Center that left a 100-foot crater. It was midnight, according to Miriam's Luminex 3000. The secret meeting called to investigate the bombing and suspects at large.

The warehouse was freezing and dark but covert enough from the public. The director of the FBI himself picked Miriam to lead this team. Low-level lights and a command center were established for the FBI Crisis Management Unit to complete their only mission: bring the perpetrators to justice.

"Are we ready?" she asked her team, who coordinated the meeting.

"Yes, ma'am," affirmed Trent Hayes, a special agent analyst.

"Everybody, huddle up. I would like to say a prayer for the victims of this tragedy before we begin our investigation," shouted Sweeney. Agents and officers bowed their heads.

"Lord, we pray for times like this moment, that the ground beneath our feet is not stable, and we now plead for your involvement and mercy. As buildings crumble around us, we know how small we indeed are on this ever-changing, ever-moving, fragile planet we call home. Yet, you have promised never to forget us. Today, so many people are afraid. Our citizens of New York hear the cries of the injured amid the rubble and roam the streets in shock. Wails of grief are for the loved ones confirmed missing or dead.

Comfort them, Lord, be their rock. Our help is in the name of the Lord, Who made heaven and earth. Blessed be the name of the Lord, Now and forever. Amen."

"For those who don't know me, I am FBI Chief of Counterterrorism Sweeney, and I will be running this investigation. If you believe you have any suspects, evidence, leads, informants, or anything else, you will run it by me first," she announced, drawing in a deep breath.

Nearly 20 FBI agents and analysts gathered to discuss the case and assignments. Along with the agents were several New York Police detectives and New York State Police to collaborate with the agency.

"When I call your name, step forward," Sweeney said. "Moore, Alvarez, Hayes, Thompson, and Deutsche."

Sweeney cupped her hand and waved it toward her to get them to follow her to the command center. There was a sizeable clear board with names in marker written down and pictures of suspected Jihadist terrorists.

Special Agent Nelson Moore turned to his former field partner, Sunny Alvarez, as they began to walk.

"How's the kid, Alvarez?" Moore inquired.

"He's active with an attitude," Alvarez replied. "You still dating that dumb red-headed bombshell you met at Gold's?"

"Hey, keep that zipped-up, Alvarez. I don't date," Moore whispered. "Intimacy issues, if you know what I mean."

"That explains everything," she said, and Moore could only hang his head and smile.

"Team, I want you to break into four teams. Moore, I want you to grab four agents and start going through items found at the bomb site. Site reviews, news footage, and speak with the attending police and responding firefighters," Sweeney said. "Alvarez and Thompson, let's start with a 1-mile perimeter and begin asking business owners' questions in the area and citizens near the World Trade Center if they saw any suspicious activity. Grab some bodies, and let's find out as much as possible and start feeding it to central."

Sweeney turned and grabbed a photo from the board and stuck it in a blue folder. "Alvarez, we believe some Jihadists might have been behind this bombing. Read the jacket and show the photo. Let's see if anyone has seen him recently."

"Got it and on it," Alvarez replied.

She turned to Wes Thompson and leaned in to speak with him. Thompson leaned over and listened.

"Wes, you're my only qualified bomb tech at this moment. I need to ensure we identify, collect, and preserve valuable evidence. Take the new robot Andros with you, or is it the Mark 5A? Just take it to the crater that was once a garage at the World Trade Center, and let's determine if there are any other booby traps left for us. Please, cowboy, no heroics. Safety first. Full body gear and Kevlar. You're in charge of this team, so bring everyone out safely."

"Chief, my men are ready. We know the drill—bag it, tag it, photograph it, and preserve lives. My team is ready to go, and volunteers will be used for analysis. By the way, nice watch, Chief," Thompson said and walked to table B to assemble his team. Deutsche grabbed his arm on his way past him.

"Good thing I am a team leader, Wes. Last time I worked with your team, you pulled that nice joke of asking me if I needed a hand," Deutsche grinned. "Of course, I wasn't expecting a victim's hand, thanks."

Thompson put some tobacco between his gums and his teeth and nearly swallowed it from getting a good laugh.

"Davis, it's only weird the first time unless someone touches you somewhere else with it a second time," Thompson said with a southern accent.

"Deutsche, round up your team, and let's interview those injured in the attack. Let's cover all the hospitals in the area. Hopefully, someone can provide key information or had a strange experience," Sweeney directed.

"Chief, family included?" Deutsche asked. He was coming into the first year of assignment with the FBI. His prior position was as a patrolman for the Washington State Police unit. This was his first bombing.

"That goes without saying," she retorted, and Deutsche headed off to brief his team.

"Excuse me, please," the man approached with caution. "My name is Shane Matthews, and I am with the CIA, Chief."

"Did Langley send you?" Sweeney asked.

"No, ma'am. I have been working with Hayes for the past few months. We had an informant we were using to penetrate a jihadist faction, which we believe may have built and detonated the bomb," Matthews said.

"Hayes," she raised her hand and motioned. "A moment, please."

"Yes, Chief," he said, looking at Matthews and knowing the topic of their last operation was out in the open.

"Why didn't you tell me about this joint operation regarding the jihadist group?" Sweeney asked.

"Excuse me, Chief, we just didn't have enough information to pin-point if this was the terrorist cell or not. Our informant had met with them as a bomb expert but could not give us enough valid information and would not testify if we served warrants for their arrests," Matthews said. "So, we let him walk."

"You let him go!" she yelled so loud that all the commotion around the command center stopped. "You know we have innocents deceased, and the count currently is 1,000 injured? And your informant walked? I almost want to tell you to both get the hell off this site, but I am inclined by duty to hear the rest of this fiasco."

"Ma'am, I have worked up jackets on each perp, and I intended to go over this after the assignments," Hayes said.

"You intended?" Sweeney said as her face turned bright red.

"Chief, we are not sure we could have prevented this bombing. The timing was complicated, and we did not have sufficient evidence. What is the target if we send him in with information to help them build the bomb? Perhaps a synagogue, and they kill someone, and agents were involved? The media would have a field day. However, we know one thing we obtained with the informant," Hayes said.

"What's that, agent Hayes?" she said with a scowl.

"We know the Chinese mafia is involved and possibly even a member of the Chinese Communist Party, an elitist," Matthews explained.

"What I can share with you is there is reason to believe a mole exists in the CIA, and now some of our agents throughout the world are being executed. We believe it is a rogue group of members of the Chinese Snow Leopard Commando Unit."

"What leads you to believe this exactly, agents?" Sweeney inquired, looking at her ex-husband's wristwatch, remembering him. He wore the watch on the arm blown off by shrapnel from an IED which killed another seal team member.

After his medical discharge, the drinking, cheating, and mental abuse killed the marriage.

"You heard about Assistant CIA Security Director Bridgewater's death?

"Yes. Dear God, Charlie's death was tragic. Are you saying his death is connected to the Chinese mafia and the Snow Leopards?" Sweeney whispered.

"In a matter of speaking, yes, ma'am. This is highly sensitive information, Chief, but I have been given authority to share this with you. When they murdered the assistant director, his autopsy photo showed the symbol burned into his forehead. An offshoot of the symbol used by the SLCU. We have discovered the same symbol on other victims.

"Nearly five years ago, a CIA operation in Tiananmen square led to the interception of a highly classified electronic device. We confiscated the device. We might say its contents are a national treasure that should never be shared. But this information was intercepted by another unidentified party. We believe the Chinese will do anything to find it."

"And how far up in the chain of command does this reach?" Chief Sweeney asked.

"Ma'am, I do not want to incriminate myself on the grounds of top-secret information that is above my clearance," Matthews warned.

CHAPTER 9

The bright sunlight was warm upon her face as the golden tinged rays reflected from her hospital window and gently woke her. Her eyelids were heavy. Her head pounded fiercely as the wall clock hands shifted with a loud click that reverberated off the solid walls of the small hospital room.

With every click, multiple beeps were coming from the medical devices, and the smell of the strong disinfectant almost made her cough. She finally began to open her eyes and tried to pull her hand up to shield her face, but it was painful because of the IV in her hand. She turned her head and opened her eyes to see a shadowed figure walking through the doorway.

"Good morning, Elizabeth," a thin, gray-haired nurse said as she wrapped the black cuff around her arm and began inflating it.

"Yes, I guess," Elizabeth said, dazed.

"It's about time, too," said the nurse whose uniform was as bright as the white walls of her room.

"Where is my regular nurse?" Elizabeth inquired. "Nurse Cynthia?"

"She is off today, and you're in my care," the nurse said as she placed the stethoscope on Elizabeth's arm and squeezed the ball violently to the point that the blood pressure cuff made her arm ache.

"I'm nurse Connard, and I will be attending to you until the next shift," she said in a high-pitched voice. Elizabeth thought this new nurse looked like a skinny bird. She had black beady eyes and a hooked nose.

Elizabeth shifted her eyes to see *9:00 a.m.* on the watch that Estelle must have placed on her wrist.

"Dr. Ellis will be here at about 10 o'clock to run some breathing tests," Connard squawked.

Elizabeth breathed in only to cough with pain. She remembered being trapped in the stairwell, living in the toxic black smoke rising from below floors. Her last memory was falling down the stairs while leading people calmly and safely to the roof. Her nurse began to speak with her, but Elizabeth tuned her out and began to concentrate on the recent events. But something was missing. Either the confusion or the nurse droning on was frustrating her. *Yadda this and yadda that.* She imagined how a typical New Yorker would describe this overbearing, loquacious, skinny nurse.

"...You are by no means to get up! If you need me, I will eventually be here to attend to you. Though, I do have a busy schedule."

"OUCH!" Elizabeth swiped her hand and knocked the IV out of Connard's hand. Blood began to spurt from her hand onto the floor and bed. The nurse was trying to stop the bleeding with gauze pads, but her white uniform and white shoes had red splotches.

"Dammit!" the nurse screamed. "I told you I would change out your IV, and now you are a mess. Were you not listening to me?"

"I'm sorry, but that was painful. And, I am not sure I like how you speak to me," Elizabeth said as tears welled up in her eyes.

Why is my memory spotty? I can remember something traumatic happened, but everything feels fuzzy, Elizabeth thought. *And this nurse! What the hell is with this old ninny?*

The nurse just mumbled and left the room quickly. A few minutes later, she returned with some hot tea, and a young lady followed her carefully, rolling in a cart with two basins.

Elizabeth sipped the tea. "Aah, that feels so good on my throat."

"Glad to see you like something, young lady," Connard sniped. "I will be training Jill, who is a student nursing assistant. We are going to give you a sponge bath."

The aide was a tall, young, beautiful brunette with short hair and green eyes. She looked more like a runway model than a nurse's aide.

The nurse slowly reversed the incline of the bed so Elizabeth was on her back, closed a curtain around the bed for privacy, and removed Elizabeth's hospital gown. The nurse pushed her cold finger on Elizabeth's bruised shoulder. The pain was so severe that Elizabeth wanted to lash out.

"I am not a pin cushion!" she quipped as her eyes began to water.

When she looked at her chest, it was black, blue, and tinged with yellow. The nurse just seemed to ignore her comment.

"Soak the sponge in one of the soapy basins and then wring it out before you begin washing her arms," Connard instructed the aide.

The warm water was soothing, but Elizabeth got cold after a moment, and goosebumps appeared on her arms.

"Okay, then use the other basin with a washcloth, rinse the area again, and dry it with the towel," the nurse said sternly and left the room to answer her buzzing pager.

"This is wonderful," Elizabeth said, smiling at the aide. "Thank you."

Jill's plump lips curled into a smile, and she meekly said, "You are welcome, ma'am."

Jill washed her from head to toe, and then turned her over to do the other side.

"Oh my!" Elizabeth got a good look at herself. "I look like a cornucopia of colors you see in a fall display at Thanksgiving."

Jill laughed. "Well, as much as those bruises might hurt, they at least match your dark blue gown," she said as she dried her with soft blue towels. The two began to laugh.

Much to her disappointment, Elizabeth could not have had her hair washed due to the stitches and bandages on her head.

"I smell like a burned piece of toast," Elizabeth stated. She could still smell the smoke, which bothered her more than the pain in her body. However, now that she was refreshed and wearing fresh, clean clothes, she felt better.

CHAPTER 10

D r. Ellis arrived a bit early at 9:30 a.m. because an earlier appointment had not shown. Dr. Michael joined her to speak with Elizabeth about what they discussed earlier that morning.

"I've arranged for another peak flow test to check your lung capacity," Dr. Ellis said. She advised Elizabeth that once they had the test results, they would provide an update.

"And will that update be sometime later today or perhaps on the next shift?" Elizabeth asked as she looked across the room at the nurse.

A smirk came across the aide's face who stood close to Connard, and the doctor gave Elizabeth a bewildered gaze.

"Not sure, but the nurse will let you know either way," she said, handing the chart to Connard. "Also, a government official is waiting to speak with you this morning. I believe he mentioned he was a JTTF Investigator. Do you want me to ask him to come and see you now?"

"Investigator? Yes, send him in, please," Elizabeth said.

Both doctors left the room to see other patients. Dr. Michael passed Estelle on the way out of the room and saluted at her. Estelle just waved him away like a captain dismissing her private.

"Auntie, how are you?"

Estelle walked in and saw her niece sitting up in bed, coherent and in better condition. She had returned with fresh clothes for her niece after taking her soiled garments to be laundered.

"Oh, my dear niece, you are my bruised peach," she said.

A rapping knock came from the open doorway, and a medium-build man with rustic features and a black coat entered. Elizabeth noticed that he had a Motorola radio attached to the left side of his belt and a Glock .40 gun on the right side.

"Come in, agent," she said.

"Ma'am, if you please, I am Davis Deutsche with the FBI's Joint Terrorism Task Force. I am here only to get a statement and ask a few questions."

"Do I need a lawyer present or...?" Elizabeth said and thought better of mentioning her handler or anything to do with the company as an expat.

"You are not a suspect, nor being charged with a crime, so I think not, Mrs. Jordon," Deutsche informed her.

"You can call me Elizabeth. Do you mind if my aunt stays, though?"

"Normally, this isn't procedure, but seeing as you don't know me and what you have been through...sure," he said.

"Then go for it," Elizabeth said, raising her injured hand.

"We have found a few injured people during the bombing, including your injuries. Did this happen when the bomb detonated?" he asked Elizabeth.

"No. I was injured during the escape from the building. I fell, I think," she told Deutsche.

"You're not sure, Elizabeth?" he asked.

"I am having some trouble remembering because I hit my head so hard," she explained.

"I have discussed some of this with the NY firemen who attended to you, and they said they found you down a stairwell," he said, pausing for a moment. "They also described a guy bleeding from his shoulder, which passed by them as they approached you. He was bent over you and looking for something."

"Huh?" she replied. "Looking for what? I don't remember this at all."

"I wouldn't imagine you would. But we believe we have an idea of who might be behind this attack. I can't go into this because it's classified, but if we could get a description, this would help," Deutsche said and continued.

"In addition, during our investigation, a .38 revolver was discovered lodged in the corner of a doorway on the 106th floor. Do you own a gun, Mrs. Bromwell?" he asked.

"No. Why?" she asked incredulously.

"Your fingerprints were on the gun, ma'am," he said.

"That can't be right. I don't own a .38," she retorted.

"Do you remember seeing anyone with a gun," he asked.

"Let me walk you through what I do remember," she replied.

Elizabeth and Deutsche went over the conference details, her exit from the 107th floor, and her fall for the next 15 minutes. Elizabeth only left one part out that scared her to the core. She remembered the man he described faintly but was not sure who he was or why he was standing over her. She needed to work this out independently or speak with her handler.

"Elizabeth, I can't tell you how important it might be to use if you remember any other details. This was a terrorist attack, and we intend to determine who attacked our citizens," Deutsche said, handing her his card. "If you come up with anything, please give us a call at the number on the card."

"Sure, anything to help," Elizabeth said.

"I will be in contact again soon," Deutsche said as he left the room almost running into Nurse Laveaux. "Excuse me, nurse," he said winking at her and headed toward the elevators.

Estelle and Elizabeth could only stare at each other in silence for several minutes before Estelle got up and walked over to her niece to give her a tender hug.

CHAPTER 11

Nurse Connard came in to check her vitals. "How are you feeling, Elizabeth?" Connard asked as she placed an orange Jell-O and plastic spoon on the overbed table.

A white flag moment? Elizabeth thought. *Why had she been nasty this whole time, and now that my aunt shows up, she is treating me with tender care?*

Estelle looked at Connard and smiled. "Thank you for taking care of my niece."

"Just doing my job, but thank you, Ms....?"

"You can call me Estelle," she said.

"Lindsey Connard. Glad to meet you Estelle," the nurse said with a smile.

"Can you tell me if the young doctor might release my niece into my care?" she asked Connard.

"The doctor is concerned about her head injury, so he wants to keep her under 48-hour observation. The laceration needs more treatment as well," Connard said as she inspected the bandages on her head.

"I will keep you informed on her progress," she said, looking at Estelle.

Estelle stayed until the specialist checked Elizabeth's lung function.

This test was quick and simple, Elizabeth thought. She tried not to show the painful attempts to take the necessary deep breaths while in front of her aunt. She did not want her to worry.

Dr. Michael returned and explained that Elizabeth would be monitored and tested further. The doctor noticed a frown appear on Estelle's face.

"As I promised, she will be well taken care of," he said to them both. "But some healing will need to take place before we can release her."

"In the meantime, I am sending her for some scans of her head and some updated X-rays," he finished.

Later that afternoon, Carson and Jacob stopped by to see Elizabeth. She was watching a reporter on the local news channel who stood in a hail of snow outside a cordoned-off area of the World Trade Center. She turned down the volume and kissed her husband and son.

A man entered the room and looked at Elizabeth for a moment before smiling at Carson.

"And who is this?" Elizabeth said, admiring the stranger's rugged look.

"This is Colonel Holt," Carson said. "He and I went to basic training and technical school together. We haven't seen each other in years, and Jacob and I bumped into him while grabbing some coffee today. I hope you don't mind, babe."

Elizabeth pondered for a moment. A quizzical brow raised on her face as she began thinking hard where she had seen this man before.

"Not at all. Pleased to meet you, Colonel," she responded, but inside kept asking herself where she had met him before.

"Yes, yes, me as well," he replied. "But it's no longer Colonel. That is my past life. But thank you."

"Oh, I am sorry. I didn't realize," Elizabeth said.

"No. My time serving this country was indispensable and has given me opportunities to enhance myself," he replied.

"Thank you for your service," Elizabeth said.

"Thank you. Carson was a pretty elite guy as well. You're a very lucky woman. You're married...to a great man."

Carson chuckled. "I am flattered, Cliff, and you're right, but don't butter up my wife."

They all laughed for a few minutes as the news reporter talked in the background. Her focus turned to the TV for a moment.

"Again...we are reporting that six deaths have been confirmed and almost 1,000 people injured here at the World Trade Center," he said, standing in front of a dark collapsed parking structure.

Jacob stared at his mother, who had gone silent. "Mom? Earth to Mom?" he smiled.

She shivered for a moment. "Huh? Oh, very funny, son. I am still here with you, but how awful that six people died in this bombing. I feel so lucky."

Carson looked at his wife, relieved she was okay, and grabbed the hospital remote from her hand and turned off the TV.

"Where is Janet? Is she feeling okay?" Elizabeth asked, focusing on her son.

"Baby Lizzie Ann is kicking and growing, and Janet did not sleep much. So, I told her I will be back to have lunch with her."

Hearing about little Lizzie Ann lifted Elizabeth's spirits. She was so looking forward to the birth of her grandchild.

Turning to the Colonel, Elizabeth asked him about his past and the backstory of Carson in their younger days. They talked and laughed for nearly two hours before Jacob mentioned he would have to get back to Janet.

Once they left, Elizabeth turned on the television again to watch the network news and learned about a terrorist cell of Islamic Jihadists. One picture of a terrorist with a mask caught her attention. She had seen this man before. *Where*, she thought, *and why was the World Trade Center targeted?*

Ten minutes later, it felt as if the news story was repeating. She had a stomachache learning that some people had perished in the bombing of the parking structure. She turned the channel to *Wheel of Fortune* with Pat Sajak standing face to face with Vanna White talking chicken recipes.

"We are going to break right now, and we will be back with the showdown between Larry, Gary, and Phil."

Ironically, the first commercial was all about Jesper's crispy and juicy chicken. It sounded terribly good, and her stomach almost moaned with hunger pangs.

"You can get eight pieces of chicken for just $5.99," the big and booming voice announced while flashing images of a young kid biting into a chicken leg.

She was hungry, but sleep seemed better than food. She yawned and watched as a box of biscuits appeared on the screen.

"And it comes with four large biscuits and honey butter."

CHAPTER 12

Ominous clouds lined the sky and a small drizzle of rain began to fall. The dull sounds of black umbrellas shot up into the sky like small missiles. The darkening clouds began to dump heavier rain, and thunder cracked in the distance.

Thousands of white crosses lined acres of Arlington National Cemetery along with the sliver casket with gold rods being held by U.S. Marines in dress uniform and white gloves. The attendees were less than 10—family members and some CIA officers who worked for the assistant director.

"Charles Bridgewater served his country with honor and distinction in keeping America safe," CIA Director Cookson said to the family, current and former military members, and other operation officers sitting in white chairs under a large white tent. "He did the right things for the right reasons."

Mrs. Bridgewater leaned over in her chair and cried out with grief. Her son's tiny hand rubbed her back and her daughter grabbed her tightly around the waist. When she leaned up, her long black hair hid the red rings forming around her eyes and the flowing tears. Two Marines handed her the folded American flag and gave a very slow salute. She let out a wail which was covered by a volley of rifles being fired to honor the fallen solider and officer. The gunfire made her jump and shake.

Meili laid her husband's distinguished intelligence medal across his casket, and her children placed a large wreath on top. Once laid to rest, Meili and the children were driven to a safehouse.

Bridgewater's wake was held at a dive bar frequented by other analysts and operation officers in the Langley area. The bar was loud with music and some patrons watching a Sweet 16 March Madness college basketball game—Georgetown vs. Syracuse. The game was tied at 35 with two minutes before halftime.

Sonya Testalov, Brad Wilson, Jason Wittcomb, and Frost sat at a small table near the bar. Bridgewater and Sonya worked many operatives before. Wilson, Wittcomb, and Frost all trained in the field with Bridgewater at some point in their careers. There was a solemn silence and blank stares.

"Can I get you a drink?" the bartender said. He was a tall young man with long black hair, and a facial scar partially covered by his clean-cut beard.

"Da," said Sonya, fixing her eyes on the young, handsome bartender who perhaps was 26 or 27 years old. "Vodka, thank you."

"Straight or on the rocks?" the bartender asked.

"Straight, strong and hard," she said.

"Order up," cracked Wittcomb. Sonya fixed her eyes on him and smiled.

"Sorry, stud, I like my men with a mane," Sonya retorted. Wittcomb was balding just like his father had at 43.

"And the knives are out," said Frost, and everyone just laughed.

"Barkeep, got a bottle of Wild Turkey?" Wilson asked.

"Whole bottle?" said the bartender, whipping a piece of his hair back from his face.

"Uh-huh, and four shot glasses," Wilson said.

They raised the shot glasses, and Wilson toasted Bridgewater as a great mentor, field agent, and friend to all of them.

"To the Wild Turkey," Wilson said. All of them clinked the glasses together and drank.

From the bar, a chair swung around, and a large balding man with glasses slid off the stool and walked over to the table. He searched all the faces of those toasting the fallen officer and sneered.

"Good evening, agents," Wilkerson said with a drunken slur.

"Kenneth, how are you?" Wittcomb asked.

"How do you think I am?" Wilkerson said, slamming a 20-ounce beer mug on the table, soaking Wilson. "Miserable, you fool. I flew from China just to attend the burial of a demon who nearly ruined my career!"

"Wow," Wilson shot up from his chair as Wilkerson grabbed his mug and walked away, headed for the exit of the bar. "Hey, numb nuts, who let you out of your cage?"

Wilson had an empty shot glass in his hand and cocked his head back to throw it, but he was stopped by Sonya grabbing his arm.

"No good, Jason," she said calmly. She was a stunning older woman with long silver hair, and she wore a red cheongsam dress with a split, which revealed her toned right thigh.

The bartender walked up with two towels. One he handed to Wilson to dry himself, and the other he used to try and mop up the mess. He couldn't help but notice Sonya's figure in the tight dress.

"Thanks for stopping your partner from throwing that shot glass," he said with his eyes fixed on her large breasts as if he was undressing her in his mind.

"You're welcome. No trouble at all, young man," she said, smiling. She leaned over and whispered near his ear, "I have nice eyes, too."

Frost slammed back his beer and let out a snort. Everyone at the table, including the bartender, fixed their eyes on him. His face was beet red, and a little beer came out of his nose. The rest came out on the table as he began to laugh uncontrollably. The only thing keeping the whole bar from hearing the conversation was people singing to the Elvis song, "Hound Dog."

"Nuts?" Frost got out and began laughing again. Sonya's eyes had widened. "His cage was open alright."

Frost nearly fell out of his chair, and Wilson, who was still drying himself off, also began to chuckle and laugh. Frost had tears in his eyes and looked at Wittcomb and Sonya.

"Wilson was right," he said, holding back his laughter. "He went commando, and his zipper is down."

Both Sonya and Wittcomb laughed and all four shared another drink before Sonya headed out for a smoke.

As she exited the door, the large red and green neon sign that read *LUCKY'S* lit up the darkness for a moment, and then it was dark again. She had a moment to ponder the events that had just occurred—Teddy being killed, the bombing of the World Trade Center, and she just received a text earlier that Elizabeth was in the tower. The emotion overwhelmed her, and a tear rolled down her cheek.

She struck a match to light her Marlboro and a few yards away noticed a drunk Wilkerson leaning against a wall with his head down, puffing on a cigar. She wiped her face with her sleeve.

"I'm sorry for that outburst," he said, looking up to meet her eyes. "Teddy was a friend but made so many enemies along the way."

She walked closer to him, and the neon sign lit up again. She looked at him with pity. The darkness lit up the red end of her cigarette, and she breathed in.

"Zip it, Wilkerson," she said, letting out a large puff of smoke.

The cigar dropped out of his mouth.

"What did you say?" Wilkerson said, almost shocked. The sign illuminated them both.

"Zip up your pants, Ken," she said, pointing at his midsection.

"Uh, ah shit," he quipped as he found the zipper with his fingers but was so intoxicated that he nearly fell over trying to pull it up. Just as the sign lit up again, he accomplished the feat of zipping his trousers. He leaned over, stumbled, and picked up the lit cigar.

"You have no idea what Charlie did to me, do you?" he whispered.

"I'm sorry that he tried to ruin you somehow," Sonya said empathetically.

"He humiliated me and with good intelligence I brought to him. He used it to kill..." his voice trailed off. "And, now, I have to sit in front of our intelligence director tomorrow to provide a report on our investigation of the latest killings and the man I served."

"Forgive me, Ken, but look at yourself. Is this really helping the situation?" she asked.

"No. But if it weren't for the former director of intelligence, I wouldn't have this position in Hong Kong—no thanks to Charlie, who was against it. For shit's sake, we served together in the military!" he shouted.

"Kenneth, let the man rest in peace!" she exclaimed. "I know that feeling of loss too well."

"Not like this," he said.

"Truly, your remarks were uncalled for in the bar, and you're embarrassing yourself with all of this anger and rage over some bad history."

"Rage, rage, against the dying of the light," Wilkerson said as, ironically, the bar light made a slight hissing sound and lit up. Sonya was very close to him now. She looked intensely into his eyes.

"Hoyas! We're number one!" two patrons screamed in unison as they slammed the bar door open.

Both Wilkerson and Sonya diverted their attention to the two men each wearing a Georgetown bulldog jersey and singing out of tune.

"Lie down forever. There goes Old Georgetown."

This reminded her of the recent events in New York. She had almost lost a second team member who she trained. Elizabeth Bromwell was young, impressionable, educated, and caught on quickly. The expat Bromwell was great at creating disguises and dedicated herself for several weeks with Sonya to learning pieces of Kenpo, Krav Mav, and some Tae Kwon Do. She was clumsy, but decent.

When the training was done, they spent time in the field, and she visited Elizabeth in the U.K. and met her husband on his birthday. Elizabeth had wanted to buy him a watch to replace an old Seiko that had seen its last days. Sonya had just seen a watch in London near their field office she thought might fit the description Elizabeth was looking for, and so they traveled to London for a day of shopping, had it engraved, and then Sonya had to catch a flight back home.

"I wonder how Bromwell is doing after the bombing of the tower in New York?" she said to Wilkerson as she stared up into the cold black sky full of burning gaslights.

No answer was returned, and when Sonya turned back to where Wilkerson was standing, he was gone. She could make out his shadow on the sidewalk lit by the streetlights ahead.

"Do not go gentle into that good night," she whispered.

"What was that, Sonya?" Wittcomb asked, standing close to her.

"N-Nothing. Just something from Dylan Thomas," she remarked as she dropped her cigarette on the ground and crushed it under her shoe.

"You okay? A lot of crazy students here tonight," he said.

"Yeah, I'm fine," Sonya replied.

"Yes ma'am, I can see that," he replied sarcastically. "The guys were giving me a hard time. I lost my date."

"Grow some." She smiled and pushed him toward the door. "Let's go, Romeo."

CHAPTER 13

The low vibration of the tool cutting into his skin was exhilarating. The artist applying the ink was a heavy Asian man of 280 lbs. He wore an Iron Maiden shirt, which did not fit, and his belly hung out. Several of his teeth were missing, and tattoos covered his body. He smiled as he placed another black circle into the middle of the leopard's body.

"Your whiskey, commander Xuebao," the artist's assistant said, holding a bottle of Jim Beam.

"Thank you, bitch," he responded. He leaned up, took a puff of his cigarette, and peered at her large, tanned breasts. He tipped the Jack Daniels bottle back and chugged nearly half of it, showing the Chinese Leopard's tattoo of death on his inside wrist.

The artist handed him a convex mirror so he could see the artwork on his back better. He leaned back in the chair, took another swig, and looked over the tattoo. The commander was one of the most feared assassins of the Snow Leopards. He spent two years training with the Snow Leopard Commandos and became a counterintelligence spy and feared killer. The many spots on the tattooed leopard represented each kill.

"Sir, are you pleased?" The artist pointed at the leopard and the newest spot.

"Yes, but on his teeth, I want dripping blood," the commander instructed. "Also, bring me some blow and make it snow."

The assistant had appeared again and dropped the white powder on a mirror laying on the table in front of him. She then took a razor blade to scrape each granule into a straight line. She handed him a dollar bill which was rolled tightly. Just as he was about to take a snort, one of his crew approached with a phone.

"Clear the room," the commander said with gritted teeth. "What is it?"

"Wǒ de mìnglìng shì shénme?" the deep voice on the other end of the phone said.

"Speak in damn English!" the commander screamed through the phone and snorted the long line of cocaine. "Is it done?"

"Yes, but...no sir," he replied carefully. "We were not able to locate the information from our target and were interrupted by the FBI and firemen in the stairwell of the twin towers."

"Congratulations on creating the distraction with our Islamic friends. The U.S. will consider this Middle Eastern terrorism," the commander beamed. "General Xie will not be pleased the investment in finding Harbinger failed."

"I accept my punishment as a PLA member. How many cuts should I take?" he asked.

"Three should be fine," his commander said. "The pain will remind you to not fail the cause again."

"It shall be done," he answered and took his knife and cut a slice into his hand. "We have been tracking an officer which matches the photo taken in Hong Kong."

"I don't care how you find it. I want the information they stole!" he screamed through the phone and slammed his fist onto the mirror, which sent glass flying.

"Yes, we will find it and destroy the information as you command," replied the double agent with a shaky voice. He knew failure would end badly for him.

"And Langley?" he asked.

"Still on point, sir," the agent said.

"Much better. Let me know when you have secured Harbinger," he said.

He closed the flip phone and yelled at the top of his voice, "Get me a mirror and a damn bottle!"

At that, the artist came in and handed the commander a mirror and a bottle of whiskey.

"Finish it," he demanded and laid back down on his stomach.

On the ceiling was a larger mirror, and he held the small mirror to reflect his entire back. The reflection showed the giant leopard with long fangs and one paw with sharp claws. Below the paw was a bear that dripped with blood. The bear's head was turned, and its tongue was laying outside of its mouth. There was an "X" in each eye, and carved into the skull was his signature marking.

"Killer," he smiled and emptied the bottle.

CHAPTER 14

On the third day, Dr. Michael met with the family to update them on Elizabeth's progress and discuss her rehabilitation with them.

"We have put together a rehab program for Elizabeth," Dr. Ellis told them. "Would it be possible for her to stay somewhere close to the hospital? This would help immensely as most of the rehab will be here at this hospital. It would also make it easier for the family if she is close by."

Aunt Estelle piped up and said, "I have a large apartment with four bedrooms that is close to the hospital. She can stay there as long as she needs to, during her rehabilitation and afterwards, if she so desires."

"Agreed. We will be able to assist in her recovery," Carson said, although he thought it would not be easy to keep Elizabeth from wanting to get back in the field. "I could hang around for two or three weeks, but then I must return to Singapore."

Estelle nodded her head.

"We will possibly be able to discharge her tomorrow, but prior to that, we want you to meet her rehabilitation team in the morning. This team, a physical therapist and an occupational therapist, will help in her recovery and teach you all, as care givers, how you can work with them to assist with her recovery," the doctor said.

"I also believe the shock of such an accident warrants some time with a mental health counselor. Most bombing victims experience night terrors or post-traumatic stress disorder," he continued.

Later that day, Estelle and Carson met with the rehab team and felt secure that they could make the rehabilitation plan work.

The next day, after a grueling schedule of rehab, Elizabeth was met with a smile by nurse Cynthia.

"Cherie, you look great!" Her enthusiasm startled Elizabeth.

"Thank you. I can say I am so tickled and relieved you are attending today. I have so much to tell you," Elizabeth snickered.

For the next 20 minutes, Elizabeth shared her experience in attending the conference. The bomb went off, and people scattered, screamed, and were panicked.

"Cherie, you are so lucky you weren't killed," Nurse Cynthia exclaimed.

"Most certainly. But that fall was not graceful. And if you didn't know, I am a bit of a klutz," Elizabeth chuckled and grabbed her ribs in pain.

"However, I feel like there is something missing in my story," Elizabeth continued.

"Whatever do you mean Cherie?" Cynthia inquired.

"I mean, I feel like I am forgetting something. I can't remember climbing the stairs and when I actually fell," Elizabeth said, embarrassed.

"Honey, you hit your head, and this was a traumatic event that may take some time to sort out," Cynthia said. "We will work on this with you."

"Thank you," Elizabeth replied.

"Okay, time for you to get some rest. I got some other rounds." She smiled and pulled up the covers, and took one more blood pressure check.

CHAPTER 15

The next day, Carson came to pick up Elizabeth from the hospital. He brought her some new clothes and a suitcase to pack up the items that Estelle had left for her.

Elizabeth, though bruised and battered, looked beautiful, he thought. As he cleaned up and packed the items on the rolling aluminum table, he noticed a pad of paper. His wife had circled Cliff Holt's name with a question mark at the end.

"Why did you...?" he started to ask before he was interrupted by Dr. Michael putting his hand on his shoulder.

The doctor had seen Carson walk into the room and wanted to share some details regarding Elizabeth's chart, provide him with instructions for her home care, and provide the release forms to sign.

"Elizabeth, you have met with the team you will be working with in your rehab. They have made their assessment and given you the OK to be released," Dr. Michael said. "I have your schedule for rehabilitation. Carson, will you take these instructions and her schedule, please?"

"Certainly," Carson said.

"I know your goal, Elizabeth, is to get back to your life as it was before. You might have good days and bad days in your rehab, but I know that with your spirit and fortitude you will make a great recovery. Just be patient, and don't push too hard," Dr. Michael warned.

"Oh, don't worry, Doc, if I know my wife, she will push herself to failure and get back and do it again. The therapist will have to keep her down," Carson said, grinning.

Elizabeth responded, "Just keep it up, buddy, and you will be getting some therapy as well."

Carson looked at the doctor with concerned eyes and raised brows and covered his mouth with his hand. With a low voice and sarcastic tone, he muttered, "As you might have guessed, she is a pistol and enforcer."

The doctor laughed. "All kidding aside, before I release you today, I have a few more tests we need to do to be able to release you, okay?"

"Sure," she said.

Elizabeth was due to have a second round of X-rays and peak flow tests before going for her physical therapy session.

Once the tests were completed, they went to the hospital café for coffee while they waited for her physical therapy appointment and the results of her tests. They sat in a corner booth where Carson raised an issue that had been on his mind since the events in the North Tower, which had led to Elizabeth's accident.

"Honey, you know I love you and that I hate the idea of leaving you here, but I have to go back to work," Carson said.

"I understand, but I don't want you..." She stopped, knowing she wanted him here but also needing to stand on her own two feet again.

"Wait," he said, holding up his index finger to purse his lips. He was trying to find the right words. "I know you love your work in the media, meeting interesting people and visiting different places in the world, but I miss you so much when you are away."

Elizabeth reached across the table and grabbed his large hand and smiled. *His hands were always so warm,* she thought. Her thoughts ran wild for a moment. She wished they could find an unoccupied hospital bed. She could dress up as a nurse and Carson would be her patient. She would treat his desires with her love potion as he held and kissed her passionately.

"When Jacob called and I saw the bombing on the news, I thought..." He stopped. His eyes welled up, and he let out a deep breath.

"Uh-huh?" she encouraged. She had a wry smile and bit her lip. She shook her head as if to clear her mind. Reality came back into focus.

"Six people were killed in the north tower that day. You could have been one of them. The thought of losing you..."

"Carson, I'm right here," she replied, trying to reassure him. "I was just in the wrong place at the wrong time, that's all. It could have happened anywhere, even in a shopping mall in Singapore."

Elizabeth knew this wasn't entirely true. The feeling was overwhelming that this bombing was intended to send a message. But what? Why did she feel she had a target on her back? She frowned.

"I want you to be at home with me. Please, please, think about giving up work," Carson pleaded. "We could have a wonderful life if we were together all the time. I dream of coming home to you each day."

His words touched Elizabeth and her heart felt as if it fluttered.

"Sweetheart. You are my protector, caretaker, and lover. I appreciate your concern, but I have faith in my skills and abilities."

When they returned to the doctor, he showed them Elizabeth's X-rays taken of her arm and ribs.

"It appears that everything is healing, and the doctor says your breathing is much improved," Carson mentioned as they drove back to her Aunt Estelle's apartment.

Carson was silent on the rest of the drive to Estelle's apartment located in the suburb of Bronxville. This seemed like the perfect location for Estelle. Bronxville is a pretty, one-square-mile village in a town in Eastchester County, only 15 miles northeast of Midtown Manhattan.

When they arrived, Carson stopped the car in the driveway. He met Elizabeth's eyes and smiled.

"What's with the cheeky smile?" Elizabeth asked.

"Well...I have been thinking," he said.

"Haven't I mentioned that can be a dangerous habit, Carson?" She grinned.

"Ha...Ha...it is kind of fun to scare you. On a serious note...do you like peaches?"

"Yes, why?" she asked.

"Maybe peaches with ice cream and pecan pie?" he said with a grin and a sparkle in his eye.

"Really?" Elizabeth knew the answer. "Stateside?"

"Uh-huh." He glanced up at the front door and noticed Estelle standing with the door open.

Elizabeth's thoughts wandered back to San Diego. This was Carson's first assignment with Leigh and Sports Leisure Company. For 20 years, Carson created or reengineered golf courses. Without their assignment in the U.K., she would have never met Lady Avebury and become an expat spy in the radio broadcasting business. And, she would not have her relocation business. They had traveled internationally for years, which could be a welcome change.

"This would be a promotion, darling, in Savannah. Leigh and Sports Leisure are being asked to renovate one of the oldest golf courses in Georgia, and well... We need time to spend with our new grandchild."

She leaned over and found his lips. "Let's do it!"

He jumped out of the car, went around to the passenger side, and lifted her into his arms. She grabbed his neck tightly, and Carson walked up the stairs of the four-bedroom Tudor home and placed her in a chair.

Carson made his family's favorite meal—tomato soup and grilled cheese on Texas Toast—when they settled in. They ate on dinner trays in bed while watching WABC's Channel 7 news. There was a storm rolling in, and the weatherman predicted New York City would see 10 inches of snow by late afternoon the next day. They fell asleep to a late-night game show.

Carson slept close to Elizabeth all night. She awoke from a dream of them lying on the beach and laughing as they sipped piña coladas. The sun's warmth on her tanned skin and the ocean breeze was refreshing. In waking, she tried to lean over and kiss Carson, but the pain of her injury stopped her. She missed his arms and wished she was in them now. Then, as if by a stroke of fate, he rolled over and put his arm over her. Her next memory was the haze of awaking in a dark bedroom and the silhouette standing over her. She froze.

CHAPTER 16

Elizabeth looked out her bedroom window and saw children playing in the next yard over, building a snowman and throwing snowballs at each other.

Estelle's apartment in the suburbs was much larger than she imagined, with a formal dining room, living room, large kitchen, two bedrooms, and a maid's suite, though Estelle did not have a maid. Estelle, therefore, made the suite an office.

Estelle had called earlier and left a voicemail. "I wonder what the surprise is all about," Elizabeth said aloud. She grew excited thinking about it. But, then, her thought process transitioned to her husband.

Carson had to leave the following day to go back to Singapore. This brought a tear to her eye. She knew he could not stay any longer, especially since his most significant project was late to the client. They knew that they would not see each other for three weeks but that they would talk every day.

"I love you, sweetheart," he whispered into her ear and gave her a light kiss. And, with that, he was gone to the airport.

The morning time of 9 a.m. flashed on the digital clock as Elizabeth lifted her head from her pillow and became annoyed by the staccato four-beep pitch. She couldn't reach it with her casted arm still in a sling. The door burst open, and Elizabeth nearly jumped out of bed.

"Hey, Cherie! Surprise!" Nurse Cynthia stood in the doorway with her hand on her hip and a stethoscope around her neck.

Elizabeth stared at the figure in the doorway. At this moment, she was filled with joy and pain. Oh, the pain. She thought it was bad today.

"What? Are you...following me, nurse Cynthia?"

Estelle walked around the sizeable jolly nurse and exclaimed, "My dear, I could use some help in getting you back on your feet. Nurse Laveaux is a licensed home care nurse I have hired."

Money was no object to her eccentric-but-so-loving aunt.

Elizabeth and Cynthia discussed plans for her recovery. Gradual steps would be taken on each visit, and they went over the week's schedule. Cynthia stayed for a few hours and had lunch with Estelle and Elizabeth. The topics were endless, and it kept Elizabeth from focusing on Carson, her career, and her pain.

"So, let's get to work, young lady, in getting you all mended," nurse Cynthia said with a large grin.

CHAPTER 17

Carson felt a sense of guilt walking out that morning to catch his flight at the John F. Kennedy Airport. The drive was a good hour away, and a yellow cab waited to take him. He was impressed. He thought this many cabbies never seem to be on time, especially at 0500 hours.

The morning sky was darker than usual, and foul weather was forecast. A cauldron of clouds and enormous thunder sounds spilled over with ice cold hail pelting the window and body of the yellow cab. Carson hurried to the cab, where the driver was holding the door.

"Good morning, sir," the black cabbie with a heavy accent said with a smile.

Carson had never met such a polite cab driver.

"Yes, good morning to you," he replied, entering the backseat with his briefcase in tow.

The cab driver walked over to grab Carson's luggage and put it into the trunk, then got into the driver's seat.

"Where are you headed, sir?"

"To JFK, please, for a very long day," Carson said sarcastically.

The ice bombs turned to snow along the way. Carson remembered his time in the military in Colorado where the winters were frigid. He could remember having to shovel his way out of his driveway. He was glad to be living in a much warmer climate now.

The driver snapped him out of his thoughts.

"Where will you be traveling to?" the driver said.

"Oh, well, uh, Singapore," Carson said.

"Very warming there, sir." The accent was undeniable, but Carson had to ask.

"Have you lived in New York for very long?"

"Almost a year now from Mother Russia," he chuckled. "The homeland is impoverished right now, and America...she's been good to me."

Carson had never met a black Russian man before. He was polite, spoke English very well, and seemed to have a good sense of humor. Carson noticed his driver ID affixed to the dashboard. *Sergei Rusmunov*, it read.

"You can call me Serg or Sergei," he said.

They spoke for the next 15 minutes on an array of subjects. Carson learned that Serg loved history and music and was passionate about American baseball. He was an instant Yankees fan.

As they neared the airport, the wind blew violently, and a blanket of snow covered the expressway. Cars began spinning out in front of them, and Sergei calmly avoided them and kept going. Carson felt alarmed and had a look of concern.

"Do you like jazz?" asked Sergei, looking at Carson in the rear-view mirror, remembering his childhood. He and his mother spent hours listening to the radio. She educated him in several genres—classical, soul, jazz, '50–'60s rock, and pop. Even old movies like *Casablanca*.

"Yes, in fact..." He stopped. His eyes widened, and his eyebrows shot up. Sergei saw it ahead, and this time, he felt a twinge in his stomach. A semi-truck heading in the other direction began hydroplaning and lost control of its trailer. The large trailer was headed right for the cab. It was so close that both men could read the painted advertisement on the side: *Dream Cakes: A Creamy Delight with Every Bite!* The trucker tried to overcorrect. The truck disconnected with its trailer and overturned, launching the trailer like a missile directly at the cab.

The large steel box swept across the lane on its side with sparks flying. At about 20 yards from impact, Sergei yanked his steering wheel left, and the G-force pulled the men the same way in their seat belts. Carson's briefcase went airborne and smacked the window. The cab was now drifting parallel and passing the trailer.

Carson's mind would later replay this in slow motion. The sight and sound of this event reminded him of an air show with two Thunderbirds heading for one another, with one flipping over at the last minute and going underneath the other at supersonic speeds.

The cab came to a complete stop, and both men saw the trailer hit trees on the side of the road and burst open like a pinata. Plastic wrapped cakes spilled across the freeway.

"Are you hurt, comrade?" Sergei said in a concerned voice.

Carson's eyes were as big as saucers. His heart was pounding, sweat pouring off his brow and adrenaline pumping through his veins.

"Holy shit!" he yelled in a higher voice than intended.

Carson stared into Sergei's eyes, which looked bloodshot and relieved. They sat for a moment until Carson noticed something in his peripheral vision which made him turn his head. The semi-cab on the other side of the freeway had also flipped over and the engine was on fire.

"Hold on!" Carson yelled, staring at the man who held his arm out of the cab.

Carson released his seat belt, opened his car door, and bolted out of the cab. He ran across the roadway, jumped up on the side of the burning truck, and yanked at the driver's door. The door swung open, and Carson pulled his small bowie knife from its sheaf around his ankle and cut the driver's seat belt. He grabbed the man's jean jacket and pulled him out safely from his potential tomb. He dragged him to a safe distance from his truck. The truck driver had a gash on his head and looked at Carson.

"You okay?" he asked the driver.

"Yep. Everything but my pride," he said with a southern drawl. "Appreciating you all the same. I almost became barbecue. Thank you."

The freeway was jammed with traffic. People gawked at the fire and the now frozen dessert cakes in the heavy snow. A man ran up with a blanket and said he was an EMT who had just finished his shift.

"I just called it in," he said to Carson. He was carrying what looked like a small piece of luggage with a red cross on the side. When he opened it, it was full of medical supplies and equipment. "I saw the whole thing. Never seen anything like that, and you're gutsy. You are a great responder. Fire and a bus will be here soon. It looks like we need to get this head wound dressed."

CHAPTER 18

Carson was drenched from the falling snow. He was exhausted from the workout involved in saving the truck driver. His pressed suit was now wrinkled, stained with blood, the smell of fuel, and sweat. In the distance, the sky lit up with red streaming lights headed toward them.

He walked up to the cab to meet Sergei for the second time this morning.

"You were spectacular, Mr. Carson," he said with a large grin. "I am proud to be your driver. No charge for this ride."

"Are you kidding me? I am astonished at your driving skills. You saved both of us from being demolished!" Carson extended his hand to him. The two shook hands. "Thank you."

Sergei then reached over and popped open the glove compartment and pulled out a bottle with clear liquid and two red Dixie cups and filled them. He then looked at Carson, put his index finger up to his mouth, and handed him the shot.

"We celebrate, no?" Serg smiled. "We live another day. This is homemade Russian vodka. I only use this when celebrating or with a beautiful woman."

At first, Carson waved this off but then realized this would be an insult. Besides, he had earned this drink. He was sure the rest of the day had much more to offer.

"Why not!" he said, grabbing the cup and then pushing it to touch Serg's lightly. "What is that you all say? Prost!"

They both laughed hardily.

Only a mile to JFK, Serg pulled over at a convenience store, and Carson went to the bathroom to change. Not many people were in the store, but the two girls behind the counter stared at him when he entered. He heard a snicker.

Looking in the mirror, Carson understood why. He had bloodshot eyes. His shirt was untucked. His hair was wet and styled like a mohawk. His zipper was down, and the back of his pants was split open.

"If Elizabeth saw you now, she'd probably laugh along with those two girls," he said aloud.

"Who is Liz, young fellow?" came a slurring voice in the closed stall. "Are the girls here? Because I got a surprise for them."

Carson could feel the blood rushing to his face with embarrassment. He stood in the first of the three stalls and quickly changed into new pants and a polo.

"That's funny, man," Carson chuckled.

The smell coming from the far stall was rancid, he thought.

"From its smell, I guess you really are talking out of your ass."

The man flushed the toilet, and it began to overflow. Carson had just put on his shoes, so he left the bathroom quickly.

Walking out of the store, one of the girls wished him a great day.

"I'd say the same, but with the gift your other patron in the bathroom is leaving you..." he replied as he walked out the door.

CHAPTER 19

The dark skies hovered over JFK airport, and the snow blanketed the runways. Carson had arrived at the airport ahead of schedule, thanks to Sergei.

"Do svidaniya." Sergei handed Carson his bag. "You have a better day, my friend. And, if you need a ride back when you return, ask for driver 669."

Carson shook his hand and walked into the main terminal to Sing Air, got his ticket, checked his bags, and headed to the nearest bar.

He bummed a cigarette off the bartender, lit it up, and took a long drag. He ordered a Seagram's and 7 Up on the rocks and told the bartender to keep an open tab. The bartender obliged but pointed out he was in the middle of a shift change.

These past few months were like a roller coaster at a fair. He was about to become a grandfather. His wife was nearly killed in a bombing. He was exhausted from sleeping in an uncomfortable bed at Estelle's for a few weeks. There was a blizzard coming to New York, and the accident was an ominous start to a long day. Once home in Singapore, he had to organize everything for the movers to pack their belongings and ship them to Georgia.

"Would you like another round?" the young blonde bombshell of a bartender said in a high-pitched voice.

Carson gazed out the large windows as the planes lined up, waiting to taxi to the runway. Carson was amazed by the snowplows with their red lights running up and down, clearing the white powder off to the side of the tarmac, which created clouds of white smoke.

Carson felt guilty for not flying back with Elizabeth for her big event.

"What if something had happened to her?" he said aloud.

"Excuse me?" the bartender said politely. Carson heard the faint voice as he followed the red lights, hypnotized by the snow lighting up the black sky.

"Yes. I don't think I would handle that so..." his voice faded.

She grabbed his hand. "I think I can handle it," she said. "Sounds like you could use another 7-and-7."

Carson's face felt red hot, and his eyes met her eyes for the first time. The bartender was perhaps 23, with long eyelashes that complimented her blue eyes and a wide smile. Her long blonde hair revealed her large cleavage in front of her shirt. The tag pinned to the country western button-down read *Nicki*. Her hand was warm and soft.

"No. Not. Nah. I will just have some water, please," Carson stammered. He felt drunk after the two shots of pure vodka Sergei had served.

She giggled, seeing his embarrassment. "Long day, huh?"

"You could say that," he said.

"Yes, I read minds, and I see you have traveled far away from loved ones," she said as she leaned closer, her voice sounding like a Russian gypsy.

He stared into her eyes in amazement, and then began laughing so hard he snorted. She laughed as well.

For the first time in weeks, he felt relaxed. It was like therapy, being able to laugh.

And then a pang of guilt swept over him like a blanket. He was flirting with someone other than his wife, and it didn't feel right. He remembered the diner and the fun Elizabeth and he had talking for what seemed to be all night. Love had found him for the first time and had not let go.

"You know, I will have another 7-and-7, thanks," he said, a smile still on his face.

When she moved to grab the Seagram's bottle, he noticed a Yankees cap on the counter.

"You a fan?" he said, pointing to the cap.

She grabbed the hat, slipped it on, and exclaimed, "You know it!"

He loved baseball, and they talked for what seemed like forever. He told her how he coached baseball and mentored disadvantaged boys as a Big Brother. They spoke of his wife and their time traveling together.

Nicki was starstruck by Carson. "You sound like such a gentleman," she said. "I have lived with so many dead-beat boyfriends, and the last one was a beater. One day, I just had enough and fought back. Shot him dead, you know."

Carson just stared blankly into her eyes.

"Nah, just kidding," she said, laughing. "But I hit him with a golf club and knocked him out. Hole in one!"

Carson laughed. "Funny. That's the business I'm in now. I design golf courses." They laughed over one more round, and he wished this beautiful young woman a good day and life. He headed for customs.

CHAPTER 20

Wilkerson drove up to the stop light of the main entrance to the Central Intelligence Agency headquarters in Langley, Virginia. The light almost seemed like it would never turn green. He looked into his rearview mirror. The cars behind him were like a line of ants on route 123.

"Ridiculous," he said aloud and took a sip of the black coffee he purchased at a drive-through on the way over.

His mind was focused on the report he prepared for the director, which did not have much information that would please his superior officer. This information was classified and stored in a very secure metal case in the trunk of the rental car he was driving.

He took a sip of the hot coffee and lit a Camel menthol cigarette. His radio was turned low, but he could hear they were playing a Stray Cats song. Then an emergency tone came across the airwaves.

"We interrupt this broadcast," said the broadcaster. Wilkerson adjusted the volume so he could hear. "We are about to hear from the President of the United States regarding the latest events in Iraq."

A horn blasted from behind Wilkerson, and he immediately looked up to see a green light and pressed the gas pedal to enter the first of three gates. He noticed the heavily armed Marines that stood at a fortified barrier as he pulled up.

"Credentials, sir," the Marine asked Wilkerson through the window. Wilkerson rolled down the window and held his badge outside.

"Any firearms in the vehicle, sir?" the broad-shouldered Marine in dress uniform asked.

"No. I'm here to..." Wilkerson was quickly interrupted.

"Director Cookson has you on the schedule. Protocol, sir," he said and waved him along.

Wilkerson had not been to headquarters in nearly five years. The only changes seemed to be a new parking lot and a new security entry feature with two other armed gates before getting to the main building. The security team officer took his badge, reviewed it, and looked at him for nearly a minute before handing it back and waving him along.

"Sir, when you exit the building later this afternoon, you will need to hand in the badge. I will be giving you an upgraded badge to meet our new security features," the security officer said.

Walking from the Langley parking lot, Wilkerson noticed the statue of Nathan Hale—the American patriot, soldier, and spy for the continental army.

Wilkerson walked down the marble hallway. He passed over the CIA seal and past the silver stars on the wall of fallen officers before getting to the main elevators. The lobby was buzzing with support staff, analysts, and operations.

He slipped the badge into the slot of the elevator slot, and there was a significant "ding" and a green light, which lit up the inside of the elevator. He pushed the number 7 button, and the doors closed and began traveling upwards. His mind was rushing and brow perspiring over what would be said about his post and the killings. The doors opened, and a large woman was standing in front of him. This was Debbie Sawyer, the personal assistant to Director Cookson.

"Assistant Chief Wilkerson, I presume?" she said, catching him off guard.

"Yes. You presumed correctly," Wilkerson answered.

"The director will be with you in a moment," Sawyer said. "I am his assistant. I want to forewarn you that it's been a bad morning here. I would recommend seating yourself just outside of his office."

Wilkerson felt tiny next to the assistant who stood up from behind her desk. He thought she was a large woman and approximately 6'2" with low-cut black heels. She pointed in the direction he was to wait, and he complied. He sat in a leather chair outside the director's doorway.

The chair did not match the other décor but was very comfortable. Pictures lined the wall of former CIA and OSS directors. He could hear a faint mumble behind the double white doors that grew louder.

"Use whatever resources are needed for Christ's sake," Cookson screamed as he paced around his office. "I want the latest technology you can use to track down Teddy's killer."

The large doors swung open, and Cookson stood in the doorway.

"Debbie, can you get me a vodka tonic on ice," the director said as he threw open his office door and welcomed Wilkerson. "On second thought, make it two."

CHAPTER 21

The cell phone rang loudly and jarred Adeel Jabril out of his deep thoughts.

"As-salamu alaykum," the Palestinian terrorist answered with a cigarette hanging from one side of his mouth.

"Mualaikumsalam," an Asian voice responded. "Adeel, is the package en route to its destination?"

"Yes. Everything is in place for its arrival," he replied.

He thought it strange how the Chinese had hired him to do this job.

"The American infidels will feel the wrath of Allah," Adeel said with a smile and revved the engine of the armored vehicle he had stolen.

"We'll make them pay," the Asian voice said and hung up.

Adeel had missed the morning rush, and there was only one car ahead of him. He lit a cigarette, inhaled, and let out an enormous billow of smoke that filled the cab.

"There is no other God, only Allah," he chanted.

The signal ahead turned green, and the Buick ahead of him pulled up to the gate of the CIA headquarters. The young marine greeted the two agents in the Buick. Both held up their badges for inspection.

"Okay, sir. Pull forward a bit," he said. He walked around the vehicle while another marine with a telescopic pole and mirror swept underneath the car looking for explosive devices.

"You're good," the marine yelled at the two and waved his arm forward. The gate began to open, and the Buick moved through the open gate.

Adeel put his foot on the gas and slowly pulled the armored vehicle forward, stopped abruptly, and opened his driver's door. He pulled out an Uzi and fired at the Marines and agents. The agent driving the Buick was hit with several rounds, and his head slumped forward on the steering wheel and horn.

The other was wounded and leaning against the passenger window. A marine was lying on the ground bleeding, the sound of the Buick horn blasting in the background.

"Sound the alarm," the marine yelled into his radio. The wail of the attack alarm could be heard across the campus.

Adeel jumped back into his vehicle and pushed the pedal to the floor. The armored car took off slowly and gained speed before it demolished the rear end of the Buick, sending it forward through the armored vehicle barrier and on its side.

"Allah, please smile upon me as I do your bidding," Adeel yelled.

The Marines began firing their issued M-16s, but the bullets only ricocheted off the armored vehicle. Adeel pushed the accelerator, made it past the barrier, and headed through the barricaded gate toward the next station.

Checkpoint Yankee was even more fortified and armed with an M134 Minigun on a Humvee. The Marines at the checkpoint heard the alarm and gunfire and scrambled.

Corporal Lance Smith was assigned to Yankee post a month prior and every day trained with his sergeant on emergency protocol drills. Smith began to breathe short, quick breaths, sweating. His adrenaline peaked.

At this moment, the alarm sounded. He looked to Gunnery Sgt. Gene Dixon, as calls on their VHF marine-band radios came across the airwaves. They were both in their 782 gear of Kevlar helmet, flak jacket, ammunition, and M-16's with gas masks attached to their sides.

"This is X-ray Dixon, stranger danger. Stranger danger!" the call blared across their radios. "1-Klick away, copy?

"Lima Charlie," Dixon answered. "Smith, jump in the hummer and man the gun."

Smith jammed his .38 into his holster and ran out the door. He realized he had forgotten his helmet and ran back through the door, grabbed it, and headed to the Humvee.

"Smith! Get on it, soldier!" he yelled. Smith turned to see the red armored truck 300 yards away heading right at him. It was moving incredibly fast, he thought. He jumped in the Humvee, grabbed the M134 gun, and fired 200 rounds of ammo at the vehicle, but it was still headed toward him. The driver screamed with rage and plowed into the Humvee. Smith's neck snapped with the impact.

"Smitty!" Dixon screamed. He saw the young kid hanging over the M134.

"Jackass, you're mine!" Dixon had grabbed a grenade and pulled the pin, throwing it in the direction of the armored truck, which had backed away and began pulling forward to the steel barricade. The explosion sent the vehicle's front end up and back to the ground. The Palestinian bounced like a pinball inside the cab, and the package had not detonated.

"Holy shit," Dixon said. The explosion had destroyed a section of the barrier.

Adeel's head was bleeding, and his vision blurry. The vehicle surprisingly moved forward through the destroyed section. Dixon fired and hit one of the truck's tires. This didn't prevent the Armored vehicle from moving forward, but Adeel knew this would slow down his mission.

"Zebra, we have a man down and need air support," Dixon said.

The truck labored along at 20 MPH and was close to its destination. Military police cars and trucks were speeding to catch this aggressor and killer. Adeel jumped out of the vehicle and began firing at the MP's.

"Allah, my blood will be spilled in your name. As my belief in the Quran states, we shall cast terror into the hearts of those who disbelieve!" he screamed aloud.

Above him was an Army Apache helicopter out of Fort A.P. Hill that had arrived from east of the campus.

"Drop your weapon and down to the ground!" several MPs screamed.

Adeel dropped the size and held out his left hand. He lifted his right fist to the sky and smiled.

The Apache fired a missile at the truck, but before it hit the car Adeel had pushed the remote button. He was incinerated, and the blast was severe.

CHAPTER 22

The beads of sweat ran down Wilkerson's forehead and into his right eye. The sting made him wince as he sat in front of the director of the CIA. This was his first in-person meeting with the director.

Cookson was a balding man with portly features that stood at 6'4. He drank Bourbon, and his fingers had jaundiced staining from smoking his imported Cuban cigars. The wall behind his desk was his dress uniform with ranking insignia and white gloves folded over his dressy white belt encased in glass. Under the case was a book on the Vietnam War and other meritorious awards. He was a purple heart recipient and war hero.

"God dammit, Ken, how could this happen under your watch?" Director Cookson criticized him.

"Sir, after our first agent was murdered in South China, we began running investigative ops. We believe we have a double agent spoon-feeding inside information on our spies to this homicidal maniac," Wilkerson said as the drink in his hand began to shake.

"Well, I am getting much heat from several agencies, including Ben Wimely, the Director of National Intelligence. I want answers fast, Wilkerson, or I will ask for your resignation. Are we clear, son?" Cookson said. "Teddy was a good man, but that S.O.B. should have had a shadow and not try to do your job."

"I was out of the country, or I would have made sure he had a detail with him," Wilkerson said, putting his drink on the table next to him. "We don't know why the deputy director was even at that bar, sir."

"Well, if we have a double agent, we will find the traitor! Any one of our agents passing along American top-secret intelligence will be prosecuted at the highest level and will certainly face the death penalty," Cookson said. "And I mean anyone. That even includes you, Wilkerson."

There was a stunned but hurt look on Wilkerson's face. His dress shirt was drenched with sweat, and he loosened his tie as if he could not breathe.

He did not like Bourbon, but at this moment grabbed the glass like it was a shot and finished it. As he went to put down the glass, the table toppled over and the whole office shook as if there was a magnitude 4.5 earthquake.

"Sorry, sir," he said, holding the glass. A cacophony of alarms was blaring around the campus. A sizeable double knock interrupted Cookson's following statement.

"What the hell is going...enter dammit!" Cookson demanded. His administrative assistant stood with gaping eyes.

"I'm sorry, sir but you're needed right away for a security debriefing—DEFCON 4," the young assistant said.

Cookson stood up abruptly, waving his arm at her.

"Tell him to come to my office immediately!" he yelled.

Security Operations Officer Jeff Danielson entered the room.

"Wilkerson, wait outside of my office," Cookson said, walking him to the door and firmly closing it. "How bad, Danielson?"

"Sir, an aggressor attempted to infiltrate the campus. He destroyed two armored barricades, shot two marines, wounded several other security details, and killed two Army helicopter pilots who crashed after he detonated a bomb near Zebra checkpoint," Danielson said. "It was a suicide bomber, sir, and we need to contain the campus. But protocol dictates we should relocate your position."

"Slow down," Cookson said. "We need to call the local authorities, and, Jesus, we are going to have a media gong show! So, we need to secure the air space, and I will call executive staff members who will brief the president. Danielson, get your team together and execute operation GoClean."

Danielson opened the door and passed Wilkerson waiting in the lobby.

Cookson turned to Wilkerson and pointed his stubby finger at him.

"Wilkerson, I am not done with you, but we have a serious situation. You won't be leaving anytime soon, so pick up the phone and start investigating what we are up against with these terrorists killing our agents. Contact your Hong Kong team to get updates," he said and dismissed him with a flick of his yellowed forefinger.

CHAPTER 23

Carson waited at the gate, looking at the monitor to see if his flight would leave on time. It read: *TBD*. The flight on Silk Airlines was scheduled to leave at 9 a.m.; this was delayed until 2 p.m.

Once he cleared through pre-screening and showed his passport and work permit, he headed to the gate. He found a lounge with some tables and decided to work to pass the time. Carson pulled out his sketch pad. He was considered a design engineer and a scratch golfer.

At 19 years old, he won 15 college tournaments and was considered the best in Texas. He earned the nickname Texas "Two-Step" Jordon. Many in his hometown thought he might turn professional, but he just quit and joined the military one day. He would not swing a club until he played with his commanding officer during his time in the military.

The newest course design in Georgia might make Bob Cupp weep. Carson admired the designer who worked for the Golden Bear, Jack Nicolaus.

His thoughts went to this course, approximately 4.9 miles long, filled with lush trees, water, and sand. He was especially incredibly proud of the par-3 fifth hole that tied off a large hill over a body of water and the landing hole flagged on an island.

He pulled out a few colored pencils and began to sketch and color. His modifications were on the ninth hole. Off the tee box, a body of water stretched 50 yards and then a high lip where if the ball fell perfectly would roll into the fairway or a little left to a sand trap. A few hours later, he closed the sketchbook and glanced at the departure board. His flight was now scheduled for 9 p.m. He walked over to his gate and spoke to the boarding clerk.

"Can you provide any update on this flight to Singapore?" he asked.

"They are in a holding pattern due to the weather, sir," She said politely. She had green eyes, a crooked smile, and could be considered a fair-skinned Asian.

Carson looked out the large glass window. The airfield was like a graveyard. Planes across the runway had lights off and were stationary. The wind was howling and whipping circles of snow at the glass windows of the terminal. The snow on the ground was thick, and clearing it would take hours.

His stomach began to growl. He realized he had not eaten all day and dinner was the perfect solution.

As he walked toward the only restaurant in the terminal, he found a group of people standing around a television at one of the bars. This was a special report on Channel 5. A weatherman put the microphone to his mouth as the wind blew snow at him and his cameraman.

"This could be the worst storm of the century, the National Weather Service is reporting," said the tall, husky weatherman. Carson thought it odd that he was wearing a beanie on his head, was dressed in a nice white button-down, a yellow sportsman coat, a red tie, and black boots sunk in deep snow.

Approximately 20 people crowded around the color television, intently listening to Jack "Hurricane" Helms. The weatherman had transferred from Miami to the biggest market in the country.

"The highest gusts in the New York City area could be up to 75 miles per hour," he said, pointing at a chart. "La Guardia Airport, 63 mph at Ambrose Light outside New York Harbor."

Carson heard a sharp ding behind him and turned to see his flight to Singapore was canceled until morning.

"Dammit," a man next to him completed Carson's thoughts exactly. He felt as if he had been punched in the stomach.

Carson grabbed dinner at a small café in Terminal 4. He enjoyed a Reuben with potato salad. There was a discarded newspaper with oil smudges on the front on the table. At the top of the page, he noticed the paper was dated March 10. There was a story on the bombing of the towers and pictures of the six people killed by Islamic terrorists.

In a separate story, buried at the bottom of the second page, a seventh body was found in the blast. Still, the FBI had not identified the person's identity and would not comment on whether this could have been the person detonating the bomb in the garage. Carson wondered if the bomber had made a grave error in setting off the bomb too early.

His interest shifted towards the sports page, and he put down the news section. While he loved golf, his real passion was baseball and the Texas Rangers. The Rangers' 3rd baseman, Dean Palmer, seemed to be on fire against the Oakland Athletics. He had three hits, two runs batted in, and a home run leading his team to a 7-4 preseason victory.

"Do you mind if I grab that part of the paper?" a monotone voice behind him asked.

"Not at all," Carson handed him the news section. The man came around to face him. He was short, probably in his 40s with rimmed glasses and slicked back hair, and wore a bow tie and white pressed shirt.

"With the flights grounded, this could be a long night, and I haven't caught up with the news in several days, so thank you, thank you," the tiny stranger said. "Then, once I am done with the paper, I can use it to cover my eyes and block out light."

"I'm Charles, but most people call me Charlie like the character in *Charlie and The Chocolate Factory*," he said. "I am in forensic accounting. However, I also keep up with the stock market and golf. Do you like golf?"

"Uh-huh," Carson could only smile.

The man started a conversation about his golf experiences and the new clubs he had just purchased. For the next 15 minutes, Charles sat next to Carson and explained his stock portfolio and how he has been working on saving and loan scandals recently.

"Going down to work with Dallas U.S. Attorney Jallen Collwin on a bank executive making illegal campaign contributions and concealing the donations from federal regulators."

"Embezzlement?" Carson replied.

"Something along those lines....mister," he said with a Minnesota accent.

"Makes me think twice about how I invest my money," Carson said.

"You are a smart man, and I could see that from afar before approaching you," Charlie said. "You are also tall and look muscular. You must work out quite a bit."

Carson, embarrassed, could only nod. He was starting to feel uncomfortable with the conversation. Charlie was a chatterbox and a sycophant.

Carson stood up suddenly and smiled. "Nice to meet you. If you will excuse me, I have to use the restroom."

And at that, Carson hurried away with his briefcase toward the men's room.

On his way back from the restroom, he stopped at a small airport café and picked up soda. He again pulled out his sketchbook and made some notes in his planner. He then went back to the lounge and waited to hear the update on the flight. Approaching the flight counter, he spoke to an airline attendant who shared that the flight had been canceled until early morning.

Carson took off his coat and found a seat in the lounge. He had a book in his briefcase just for this occasion—*Ben Hogan's Five Lessons: The Fundamentals of Golf.*

CHAPTER 24

Cookson looked at his watch. He assembled four staff members in the conference room. Joining him were the director of intelligence, FBI assistant director of terrorism, and two other CIA head of security.

"Gents, I can't tell you how much heat will be coming my way in the next few days from the President of the United States, Joint Chiefs of Staff, Department of National Intelligence, Congressional members, and must I go on," Cookson said solemnly. "What do we know?"

"Sir, we have created a task group Gap fire *Bluff* and are working with the FBI and Fairfax County police. The Palestinian who attacked our headquarters worked for a jihadist group. However, we believe his orders might have come from a communist faction either out of China or Russia," his Security Operations officer Danielson recapped.

"We believe the attacker was Adeel Jabril based on fingerprints we were able to run from the arm left over from the bombing. There are five KIA members of Langley, and we have recovered an AK-47. Ballistic tests confirmed it was the gun used in the attack. After being worked on, the armored truck was stolen from an auto shop."

"No other assailants involved?" Cookson said with a raised eyebrow. "How did one individual penetrate so far into our defenses?"

"Separate unit on that piece of the investigation director. We will follow up on this in our next debrief, sir. However, the FBI and Fairfax police searched several gun stores and tracked down a sales slip in Chantilly where he bought the gun. We are also working with the FBI's Counter IED Operations team on the device he detonated."

"He also had a symbol branded his arm's inside below the palm. And we have seen one other brand like this in the bombing of the World Trade Center last month," Danielson ended.

"Okay, so what is the symbol, and have we run intelligence on this?" Cookson asked.

"Yes. This is the same symbol branded into Bridgewater, sir," Danielson said with a sad tone.

Cookson's face turned bright red with anger. "I want to know what this symbol means and if this a terrorist group or if Jabril ran it. If it's the latter, the threat is contained," Cookson said.

"Sir, if I may?" FBI Assistant Director of Terrorism Steven Daugherty said. "In New York, one of the NY Detectives, Davis Deutsche, interviewed a woman that is an expat working with the CIA. Are you familiar with the name Elizabeth Jordon?"

"Yes, she was recently decorated with a commendation letter for a covert mission in saving one of our agents," he said.

"In that attack, we have verified at least one CIA agent and Jordon were hurt in the explosion. There were six other field operatives injured in the attack. Additionally, we spoke with New York Fire and police and were told a man was standing over Jordon when they approached. One of the firemen said he was searching her," Daugherty said.

"But, most interestingly, he suffered an injury and was bleeding from his shoulder. The same fireman believes he saw that same symbol on the injured man's hand as he ran past him in the stairwell."

"Danielson, I want all the details in a report to submit to the president in the next 24 hours. Thank all of your teams for the quick response and great intelligence. Let's keep it up," Cookson said, adjourning the meeting.

In walking back to his office, he stopped at his assistant's desk.

"Debbie, get Wilkerson on the phone. I have an assignment for him." Cookson walked into his office shut the door, grabbed a glass, and poured a drink. He took a long sip, grabbed a cigar, bit its end off, and lit it. He sucked a long draw from it and blew a puff of smoke out.

His phone lit up, and Debbie announced she had Wilkerson on a secure line. Cookson picked up the receiver and pressed the second button on the phone.

"You there?" Cookson asked.

"Yes, sir," Wilkerson said.

"Ken, I am sorry about the interruption at our last meeting. We have a lot we need to discuss, such as what is happening in Hong Kong and what we will do in the near future," he said. "For now, I will send you and another officer to visit Elizabeth Jordon. I believe she may be in the New York area. There are some questions we need to go over with her."

"Okay, sir, but what is this about?" Wilkerson asked.

"You will be debriefed. Once I get off the phone, reach out to operations and speak with Danielson. He will have all the details of your rendezvous with the other officer," Cookson said. "Report back to me in the next 48 hours."

CHAPTER 25

Carson opened his eyes slowly and lifted his head from his chest. Staring at him was a heavy-set kid with bad acne who plopped down into the third seat of the row and consumed what looked to be a McDonald's cheeseburger. He saw a line forming at the gate, and a sense of relief came over him.

"Ladies and gentlemen, Flight 609 on Singapore Silk Airlines will begin boarding all passengers in 13 minutes," the airline attendant announced. "We will begin boarding those with senior members, handicapped, or families with small children at that time."

He looked at his watch, which read 8:12 a.m. He did not sleep well in a very uncomfortable environment. *Perhaps it was designed this way so the local hotels picked up the business of layover passengers*, he thought. In any case, the departure lounge smelled of cigarette smoke, body odor, and coffee. His attempt to makeshift a pillow out of his folded coat failed. The bench seating had a metal armrest for each chair, making it impossible to lay down. He was dead tired.

As he leaned up, he noticed a bank of telephones near the gate and decided to make a call to Elizabeth. The phone rang at Estelle's, but no one picked up, and her message machine picked up.

"Hey, guys, it's Estelle. If you're calling to take me on a date, you're late. I'm already out with someone else, but leave a message anyway."

BEEP...

"Estelle, that message gets me every time," Carson said with a chuckle. "Elizabeth, I wish I could say I was in Singapore, but my flight was delayed because of the blizzard, and we are now leaving. I will give you a call, sweets, when I arrive home."

His next call was to Jacob to see how Janet was feeling. She had been diagnosed with pre-diabetes in her 20th week. He dialed Jacob's apartment in Cincinnati.

"Hello," Janet said.

"Hi darling, how are you?" Carson asked.

"Hey, soon-to-be grandpa," she responded.

"Well, I was going to ask how you are feeling, but now, after that endorsement, I know you are feeling good," he replied.

"A little," she replied. "I'm tired of being pregnant, you know?"

"I can't imagine," he said. "Is my son taking good care of you?"

"Like a champ," she said.

"Well, my plane got delayed in New York, and it's now getting ready to board. I thought I'd check up on both of you before heading to Singapore. Have you spoken with Elizabeth recently?" he asked.

"No, the last time was when she just got out of the hospital and headed to Estelle's," she replied. "If I do, do you want me to tell her you're trying to get in touch with her?"

"I tried to call Estelle's this morning, but no one answered," he replied. "Is..."

"Jacob, your dad is on the phone, honey!" she said.

"Kisses to you and the baby. Have a great day," Carson said.

Janet passed the phone to her husband, who walked in from the backyard.

"Dad, how are you?" Jacob asked.

"Fair to midlands if there is no snow involved," he replied.

"Oh, there was a terrible blizzard in New York last night. I saw on the news," he said.

"Yep, and I didn't leave the airport," Carson said. "I am headed to the gate for my flight to Singapore. The movers are due Monday or Tuesday."

"No Bueno. I am sorry that you have been dealt a bad hand. I always hated to move," he said.

"Really?" Carson replied.

"Yeah. Packing my room up and then unpacking to a new room always got tedious," Jacob admitted. "But spending time with you learning about new places and learning how to do new things was the best. Especially the time you taught me how to surf."

"Well, I'd rather chew broken glass than pack my life away in a box, son," he said.

"Yet the traveling is just in my blood and now second nature. I enjoyed every time we spent time together."

"Miss you, Dad," Jacob said. "Have a safe flight."

"Will do," Carson said. "I will call you on my way to Georgia."

"Yep. Bye, Dad," Jacob said and hung up the phone.

Carson gathered his small suitcase and briefcase and headed over to the line for the assigned seating.

Carson's seats were in the middle of the 737, and there was ample leg room to stretch out. He was seated with a young mother and a hyper Asian child that kept asking questions.

He was prepared for the 18-hour flight. He paid for a drink with his meal and bought some headphones to watch the inflight movie, *In the Line of Fire*. Three hours into the flight, his eyelids became heavy watching Clint Eastwood as a secret service agent being taunted by a killer.

The dream was vivid. He was floating like a balloon just above a bed of water. The wind was mighty and plunged him into a river. His body whipped back and forth down the river until he reached a town. A wave picked him up out of the water and climbed on top as if he was surfing. He felt as if he would fall and had no knowledge of balancing himself. The wind became violent and turned into a tornado. He was thrown and landed on his feet in front of a church. A priest was yelling and had a cupped hand waving at Carson to come to him.

The church was on fire, and Carson tried to make out what he was crying. Carson felt his shoulder shift left to right like a doll. He felt a jerk from the plane's wheels pounding the tarmacked airstrip.

"Mister...? Wake up, Mister," said the little Asian girl sitting next to him.

"Excuse me, sir, my daughter does not know her manners," the Asian mother explained.

Carson chuckled. "Not to worry. I had a boy that age some time ago, and I never got to sleep, but thank you."

Carson looked at his Lange & Söhne wristwatch. He never wore jewelry and only had his military ring given to him by Colonel Holt during a ceremony. The wristwatch was a prized possession. A wedding gift from Elizabeth and engraved on the back was a message Carson memorized: *To My Husband, Meeting you was Fate; becoming your Wife was a Choice, but Falling in Love with you was Beyond My Control.* The watch rarely left his wrist. The time read 3 a.m., and he stretched and yawned, and a slight chill ran through his body. His feet felt numb from the position he slept in the passenger seat.

CHAPTER 26

She awoke at dawn, moved her tangled hair away from her eyes, and cocked her head to the right to see the time on the nightstand. In the room's pitch black, the digital alarm clock with light emitting diodes showed 4 a.m. in neon red.

"Eh," she winced and covered her eyes like a vampire entering the light.

Elizabeth pulled back her long messy hair and laid on her back for a moment. She focused on ignoring the pain of her injuries and became frustrated. She ripped off the white goose down comforter with her good arm like it was a bandaid. She felt a cold shiver move through her body like a jolt of electricity, which made her jump back underneath the warm blanket to recover.

"I have to get out of this house. I am so bored of lying in bed," she said with a faint whisper as if the room had ears. She planted her feet on the ice-cold floor and began to feel her way to her dressing drawer a few feet away from the bed. On top of the dresser was a small light which she managed to turn on. The light was no better than if she had lit a candle.

She searched and found some comfy sweatpants, a Van Halen T-shirt, and a sweatshirt with a hoodie which she put on slowly and methodically. She then searched the top drawer for some socks and realized she needed shoes. She moved to the closet at turtle speed and felt as blind as a bat.

"Oof," she gasped and took a deep breath after running into the edge of the wooden chair with her toe. She had built up a pain threshold and while her toe ached, she could ignore it. However, if she were trying to be stealthy, this maladroit moment would have woken the dead.

"Thankfully, I did not fall over the chair and break my arm again," Elizabeth thought. She turned the knob of the closet, pushed the door open, and walked a few steps inside. She reached up in the dark and found the string hanging.

"Click-clack," the closet light came on and hissed.

There were her Nikes that Estelle had unpacked and put neatly on a shelf. She turned off the light and carefully headed to the bedroom door, which whined at the hinges. She sat down on the first step and attempted to put on her socks and shoes. The whole ordeal was exhausting, and she considered giving up. But since she was dressed now, she picked herself off the stairs and headed down the creaky wooden stairs. Estelle's big-eyed calico was lying at the door starting at her with conviction.

"Don't you dare tell Estelle," she whispered with her finger over her tight lips.

Her next feat was to get out the front door which had two knobs. This was a safety feature to keep toddlers safe. Both knobs had to be turned simultaneously, and she had only one hand free. After a few tries, she got out the door by turning the circular knob out and then pulling on the flat knob out towards her body.

Finally, she was outside, and immediately, it was much colder.

"Brrr," she said, wrapping her arm over the injured one in the cast.

The sun rose slowly in the East, and the warm rays poured over her. She yawned and stretched and got a good look at what she was wearing.

"Hell yeah," she said in a low but proud voice as she began walking.

The sweatpants were orange and adorned by the Sarah Lawrence College hoodie with a bright yellow griffin on the front. With each step, the snow seemed to be hitting the top of her Nikes, and her feet felt cold.

"Geez, what a blunder," she said aloud.

There was a quick realization that boots would have been the better choice.

Elizabeth walked carefully so she would not slip and be further injured. She walked over a maintenance hole with steam pouring through the holes like a once-active volcano.

After 10 minutes of walking, the sun dipped behind a cloud, and light flurries of tiny white flakes blew into her face.

The chill made her body shiver and ache. A young teen delivering newspapers to houses passed by and stared as he rode by her.

"I'm good, thanks. How about you?" she regaled. Distracted by her comment, the young teen with red hair and a skinny frame through the paper off course into a bush. He turned right down another street as if escaping her platitude.

She convinced herself that some exercise and fresh air would be a revival. After a ½ mile trek, she found a café. The restaurant stuck out in the sub-urban community. It was a red, quaint cottage with a striped zebra awning and a large glass window painted in yellow cursive that read: Tag's Café.

The sweet smell of heaven pulled at Elizabeth's nostrils, and she was drawn to the glass where she could see the pastries and croissants on display. The aroma reminded her of a warm fuzzy blanket out of the dryer.

She was committed and pushed a heavy glass door to enter, but the door wouldn't budge. She went to try again and heard the door frame scraping the floor plate and let go.

"Hello. Welcome," said a young man pushing the door outward to open it for Elizabeth. "I'm Hank, glad to meet your acquaintance."

"Hi?" Elizabeth said with a dose of surprise in her voice. The young man was thin, with a long nose, broad forehead, and wide-set eyes. His wide smile was infectious.

"Well...come in and sit wherever you would like," he said, pointing at the empty tables throughout the small establishment. He then made his way around behind the counter. "Our cook makes scrumptious cakes and other goodies."

An older heavyset woman with a dark complexion, green eyes, and brown hair in a bun walked through the double doors behind him.

"I see you have met Hank," she exclaimed. "I'm Maryann, the owner of the café."

"Yes, he has been very cordial. Thank you. I'm Elizabeth. Elizabeth Bromwell."

"Did you take her order, Tag?" Maryann asked.

"No, not yet, Ma. I'm sorry, Miss," he said with the response of an innocent toddler.

"It's okay, Tag. Let's start with giving her a menu," she explained.

Tag grabbed a green laminated sheet.

"Here you go, misses," Tag said, frowning as he slid the menu awkwardly on the counter in her direction. He stood and gazed at her with an open mouth.

"My apologies. My son is just learning the business and is...well..."

"Has special abilities," Elizabeth quipped.

"Yes, he does," she said with a grin. "Autistically-inclined."

"What can we get you?" Tag shouted. "Do you like chocolate donuts? What happened to your arm?"

Elizabeth giggled.

"I was injured falling down some stairs. I am a bit clumsy," she admitted. "Do you have breakfast tea?"

"With cream or without?" Tag asked.

"Cream, thank you."

"I am sorry about your fall," he said with concern. "How about a crumpet with your tea?"

Elizabeth raised her eyebrows.

"Wow, sounds delicious. That would be fantastic," Elizabeth said with a smile. She looked over at Maryann, who seemed bewildered. She raised her palms to the sky and shrugged her shoulders.

"A breakfast tea with a crumpet coming right up," he repeated the order back to Elizabeth. He scribbled on the order pad, turned to face his mother, and handed her the order.

"Order up!" he said in a loud voice.

A few minutes later, Tag brought out her tea and a cherry Danish. Maryann followed him.

"Tag, can you clean the counter and tables for me?" Maryann said with her hand on his shoulder.

"Yeah. Sure, ma'am," Tag said with a glum look. "Not my favorite, for sure, but okay."

"Elizabeth, sorry we don't have crumpets," she said. "I hope a cherry Danish will do?"

"Certainly, I will never turn down something sweet," Elizabeth chuckled, and both of them laughed together.

After finishing the Danish in three bites, she enjoyed her tea while looking around the small café. The walls were filled with photos of local elementary and high school kids holding up trophies or lined up like bowling pins with their coaches. There was a chalkboard with the special for a day at the top in bold letters. There were gift baskets and other trinkets aligned just underneath the wired hung lights.

After reading the paper, she pushed out of her chair and slowly pushed herself up without any resonating pain. She walked up to the counter.

"That made my day. Thank you, Tag and Maryann," she said. "How much do I owe?"

"That will be $1.50," Tag whispered.

"We appreciate your business, Elizabeth," Maryann said. "Are you from around here?"

"No. I travel quite a bit. I am a radio show host," Elizabeth explained. She was interrupted by three local firetrucks headed past the café. The sirens made her jump, and the images of the bombing flooded back. She began coughing violently.

"Here is some water, young lady," Maryann said, handing her the glass.

Elizabeth drank slowly until the coughing ended and looked at Maryann.

"Much obliged for your kindness," Elizabeth said, putting down the glass and fumbling through her pockets for cash. She placed two dollars down.

"Keep the spare change," Elizabeth said. "I hate loose change rolling and jingling in my pockets."

Elizabeth waved goodbye, looking at Tag, and ran into the glass door, pushing it out and bouncing off the door. She caught herself. The young teen who was about to push it forward was now headed backward and fell on his butt.

"Sorry...?" Her face felt flush as she looked through the glass at the same teen who had been on his paper route earlier.

"No problem," he said with a squeaky voice. He brushed off his bottom, got to his feet, and opened the door for Elizabeth.

"Thank you. You are such a gentleman," she responded to his gesture

Elizabeth remembered when Jacob went through puberty. His voice cracked, he grew taller, and he started growing facial hair.

She could only think of Carson and his trip back to pack their home on the way.

She was imbued with the idea of moving to Georgia. The new role would be suitable for her and Carson. She would be closer to her grand baby, and this excited her greatly. The thought was interrupted by another fire engine passing. She could smell the smoke.

"Must be a big fire," a woman said in passing.

"Yeah, must be," Elizabeth responded.

She heard a ring and then a vibration coming from her pocket as she walked. She flipped her cell open and put it to her ear.

"Hello," she said.

"Mom, we just got home from the hospital."

"Hospital? Am I a grandmother?" Elizabeth shouted.

"No, Mom. We thought you might be a grandmother today, but it turned out to be a false alarm," Jacob said with a disappointing tone.

"Whoa! You nearly gave me a heart attack, kid!" she said, pacing. "I was nearly ready to run back to your aunt's house and have her drive me back to Ohio."

"Mom, everything is fine. We were surprised since Janet is not due for another few weeks," he said. "We wanted to call you and let you

THE CASE OF THE CHINESE LEOPARD

know, so please tell dad when you talk to him. Janet and I are going to go lay down and rest. We love you."

"Love you, bye," she replied. As she closed the flip phone, she realized she did not know where she was in Estelle's neighborhood. But she did hear church bells to the south of her direction. She remembered the Catholic church was near her aunt's house. She turned and began walking toward the sound of the bells.

She passed several streets until she passed Longwire Street and could see her Aunt Estelle on the porch in a chair. As Elizabeth approached the house, she felt she was being followed. She looked back, and there was a black Pontiac 301 moving slowly down the street.

"Where have you been?" Estelle said.

"Well, Auntie..." Elizabeth was cut off by a screech of tires and the sound of a roaring engine heading towards her. She turned to see the muscle car slam on its brakes and turn sideways, almost hitting her.

"OH MY GOD!" Estelle screamed in a methodical high voice.

Elizabeth felt the adrenaline rush she had felt in the bombing of the tower.

The passenger side door opened, and a very tall, muscular man stepped out. He was wearing a black T-shirt filled with muscle jeans and a skull belt buckle, as well as large black industrial boots. He reminded Elizabeth of a bouncer at a night club. Only much scarier.

"Get in," he demanded with an extraordinary accent.

"Are you kidding?" Elizabeth said with alligator eyes and raised eyebrows. She could feel her body shaking.

"Get in!" he demanded.

Pap-pap! The crack of gunfire sent everyone crouching.

"Listen, douche bag, get away from my girl now, or I am going to plug some holes in your large candy ass!" the scream came from the porch.

Elizabeth turned to see Cynthia holding a .38 caliber pointed at him.

"Listen, beefcake, I ain't kidding," she said and shot off another round.

"Jesus, Cynthia, stop already!" screamed Estelle, covering her ears.

A skinny, bearded man with dark, black-framed glasses emerged from the driver's side. He was a petite guy with a thick Italian accent.

"Hey, we mean no disrespect!" he shouted. "You Ms. Bromwell?"

"Yes, why?" said Elizabeth.

"This guy paid us to deliver this letter to you," the driver explained. "We're just transporters, you know. I was strictly instructed to make sure you understand the seriousness of what is contained in this envelope."

"Who gave it to you, and why is it so important?" she asked.

"This guy called us last night at our apartment. We normally move furniture, but one of our friends recommended us. So, we met him near Long Island, and he gave us the envelope with instructions," the driver said. "Apologies regarding me running my car hard at you and Frank's actions. I tried a Starsky and Hutch approach, you know what I mean?"

"You two need to work on your approach," she snarled, and walked around to meet him. She stopped on the other side of the vehicle and noticed Cynthia in pink polka dot pajamas with Ms. Piggy slippers, still pointing the gun.

"Cynthia," Elizabeth motioned her hand to have the nurse lower the gun. She turned to look down at the driver, who was trying to get her attention.

"What?" she yelled intensely, and the adrenaline pumping through her made her feel jittery.

He was a small Italian man with a long beard, and brown beady eyes. The sun was shining off his bald head as he looked up at Elizabeth.

"This is for you, doll," he said, handing her the envelope. "Name is Carmine. Glad to meet you."

"Thank you," she said with a smile and rubbed his head as if he was a dog. "Wow, I think I can predict your future."

"How's that?" he questioned.

"I see you and your ogre friend, Frank, jumping in your car and taking off now...In other words, get the hell out of here and don't come back!" Elizabeth yelled, pointing her finger toward the city.

"Frank, she is good. You see, chicks do like bald men as I told you."
He grabbed the driver's door handle, opened it, and launched himself
into the driver's seat.

"All of that for an envelope?" Elizabeth said and launched her hands
up into the air. She walked to Estelle, who was now sitting on her
wooden porch steps with her arms folded tightly at her chest. Neighbors were standing on their porches gazing in astonishment.

As Elizabeth passed Frank, she saw a large wet stain on the front of
his pants and a yellow puddle on the sidewalk. Frank noticed her gaze
and covered his hands over the lake-size stain on his jeans. He quickly
moved and got into the Pontiac and slammed the door. They peeled
out down the street past the church.

Elizabeth hugged her aunt and smiled up at Cynthia standing on
the porch.

"Thanks for having my back there, ladies," Elizabeth said, walking
her aunt up the stairs.

"Cynthia, where did you get a gun?" Elizabeth said, staring at this
new side of Cynthia she had never seen before.

"Let's just say I was a wild child growing up in New Orleans, Cherie."

"Wild Child?" both Estelle and Elizabeth said in unison.

"That's a story for another time. What's in the envelope he handed
you, Cherie?" Cynthia asked.

Elizabeth stared at the envelope in her shaking hand. She turned
it over and read the bold lettering **FOR YOUR EYES ONLY,** stamped
red. She was almost terrified to open it.

CHAPTER 27

After deplaning, Carson made his way from Terminal 2 to baggage. He was back on the island that was 22 miles latitude and 42 miles longitude. It rained 178 days out of the year, and the sun rose at 7 a.m. and set at 7 p.m.

The terminal walk to baggage was like being stuck in an arboretum. Passengers were captivated and beguiled by the exotic vegetation growing in and around Terminals 1 and 2. Carson wasn't fond of the foliage accented by mustard yellow walls. He stopped to look at the Lithops for a moment.

"Ugly, aren't they?" a voice said behind his shoulder.

"Extraordinary is more like it," Carson retorted.

"Beauty is in some beholder's eye, I guess?" said the tiny blonde Asian woman now standing by his side.

"I respect nature and beauty, Sue Tang," he said, looking down into her dark brown eyes. "The lithops mimic stones or pebbles as defense from being eaten by animals."

"Jeez, Carson, you are a smart one, aren't you!" Tang laughed at a high pitch. She was a Chinese national who began offering inside information to Carson. As a former golf pro, she was always looking for a challenge. Carson had played her once and came very close to beating her.

"Are you building any challenging courses soon I can't beat?" she teased.

"Not that I can tell you about, Sue," he replied.

"Not even one of the toughest holes?" she laughed. "Come on, Carson, it's not like I don't share my secrets."

"Why do I feel like this conversation will land me in a sand trap?" Carson asked.

"Better than the water?" Tang squealed this time. "Wait. Where's Elizabeth?"

"That may be a longer story than you and I have time for at this moment," he explained. "The short story?"

"Sure."

"She was injured falling down some stairs in New York during a conference she was attending," he said solemnly.

"Oh no, is she going to be okay?" Tang asked, concerned.

"Certainly. She is staying with her Aunt Estelle in New York, and they hired a live-in nurse to help with her physical therapy," he said. "I am supposed to give her a call once I arrive, but the time difference will preclude me from doing this until morning."

"Well, I am glad to hear things are okay, Carson. Give her our best recovery wishes, please," Tang said.

"You're up early. Are you traveling on an assignment?" Carson asked.

"Let's just say I am the babysitter on a bag and burn operation in Hanoi," Tang said with a smirk on her face.

"Who's the lead on the project?" asked Carson.

"Mulrooney is taking the lead on the project for this course," she answered and rolled her eyes. Mulrooney could be pushy and was not a team player.

"Mulrooney? He is nuttier than a squirrel turd. His malfunction in Dubai nearly got him rolled up," Carson said. "I hate to run, but the men's room is calling after a long flight. Good luck, and let's catch up sometime soon."

"See ya, Two-Step," she said with a handshake, and then walked to the departure terminal.

CHAPTER 28

Elizabeth was clearly shaken, and both Estelle and Cynthia noticed. Estelle grabbed Elizabeth's hand and led her to the couch.

"Lizzy, what is going on?" Estelle asked. She had not called her this frazzled since she was a child. "Who were those two men, and where did Cynthia get a gun?"

"Auntie, I wish I could tell you what is going on, but I am clueless!" she answered.

She turned her head and looked at Cynthia. "No more guns! Okay?" Elizabeth deflected.

"Yes, ma'am," Cynthia said with a smirk. "You okay, Cherie? You look pale, honey."

Elizabeth did not feel well, and nausea came over her. She looked at the envelope she had placed on the coffee table in front of her. She knew it was official and possibly could not be opened in front of Estelle or Cynthia.

Just then, someone pounded on the front door, followed by ringing Estelle's doorbell, which sounded like bees.

"Okay, already, I'm coming!" she yelled as she swung the door open to greet two Bronxville police officers standing on her porch – a female police officer and a chubby male officer.

"Ma'am, one of your neighbors called in a noise complaint. We hear someone might have discharged a weapon?" the female officer asked.

"Whoa, I am so sorry, officers! My young grandson was playing with his nanny. They were playing cowboys and Indians. To make it fun, she lit a couple of firecrackers to make it seem more lifelike," Estelle explained. "I scolded the both of them for this."

The officers looked at each other and then shrugged their shoulders. The overweight officer, who looked like donuts were part of his daily diet, looked at Estelle and pulled a ticket book out of his back pocket. He began writing and looked up at her.

"Lady, I have a kid at home, and I get it. I also own a television. How about you have the nanny plop the kid in front of the television and watch a good western?" he said sternly. "Us blues don't like being called out for no reason. I'm leaving you with a courtesy warning. Have a good evening now."

The officers walked to their vehicle and got inside. Estelle could see them laughing, and then they drove away.

Estelle looked across the street. One of her neighbors was an older man, Mr. Walter P. Elligan, as he introduced himself before. He had pulled back the drapes in his window and perhaps observed the whole incident. Elligan, perhaps 15 years older than she, was known as a neighborhood snoop. He earned this title after being caught using his binoculars to look into a neighbor's backyard. Perhaps he might have been the person who called the police, she thought.

"Asshole," she whispered but subvocalized it so Elligan might decipher her lip movement.

As she began to close the door, she noticed a black caprice sitting on the opposite side of the street. There were two men in the car, and one was sipping coffee. The other was reading a newspaper. A young girl approached the driver's side window. The driver rolled down the window, and the girl pointed in Estelle's direction. The driver's eyes looked right at her, and Estelle quickly closed the door, fearing it was reporters.

"Liz," Estelle called from the hallway.

"She is indisposed!" Cynthia shouted from her knees in the living room. "I guess she was quite upset seeing the police and hurled."

"Poor girl," Estelle said as she came in to see Cynthia cleaning up. "Cynthia, you don't have to do that."

"Not even a worry, Ms. Estelle. Besides, I am almost done cleaning this," she said.

Elizabeth could hear the chatter of her aunt and nurse from the living room. She felt terrible that she had to make herself sick on her aunt's wooden floor. However, she needed some distraction to read the contents of this envelope.

She slowly pulled the adhesive bi-fold and looked inside.

"Two tickets to Les Misérables?" she asked herself, bewildered. She knew it could not be Carson. He was not one for the theatre. She then opened a folded piece of paper and read it:

I heard you on the music box, and we met. The road to Oz with a carriage will arrive. The carnivore "CLTrator" is seeking IMINT. The plum blossom is the HARBINGER of spring. 0100Z WSU. Commit2mem and burn.

"Creepy!" she said aloud while opening the bathroom door and looking into her aunt's eyes.

"What was creepy?" Estelle said.

"Oh, I was just thinking about those thugs from earlier, that's all. I was just thinking about those thugs from earlier." Elizabeth replied.

"What was in the envelope?" Estelle asked.

"Well...it would seem I am going to the theatre," Elizabeth answered. "My old college friend Jennifer Brown. She must have heard I was in town, and she is inviting me to meet her in New York for a Broadway show."

Elizabeth held up the tickets, and Estelle smiled.

"How sweet! How long has it been since you saw her?" Estelle asked.

"Not sure," Elizabeth said, distracted with the message she read. She was trying to process the coded cable. "Ugh, about 10 years or so. The last I heard, she was working as a doctor for a medical clinic."

"Well...Do you have a dress for tonight?" Cynthia inquired as she walked behind Estelle.

"Were you spying on me, nurse?" Elizabeth said with a quirky smile.

"More like eavesdropping, Cherie," Cynthia said with a laugh, peering around the corner.

"No, but I got something nice I packed for my trip to New York," Elizabeth said.

"Cherie, let's go. I will drive you to find a nice dress," Cynthia insisted.

"What a wonderful idea," Estelle said. "Let me grab my purse."

"Hold on, auntie. I am not sure I need a new dress, and I don't need money. I will pay for it if I find something," Elizabeth said. "You have done so much for me already."

Estelle's facial reaction communicated defeat and sadness, and Elizabeth hated to hurt her aunt.

"Well...okay. But I don't need that much," Elizabeth said.

Estelle grabbed her purse and handed her $350. There was a glint in her eye as she hugged Elizabeth.

"Thank you, I love you so much," Elizabeth said, taking a breath. Her ribs were beginning to hurt.

CHAPTER 29

The drive to Yonkers gave Elizabeth time to try and decode this message. She knew it was either another expat, CIA, or MI5. *But who?* she thought.

"Elizabeth, did you hear me?" Cynthia asked. "Macy's or Bloomindales?"

"Yes, sorry. Macy's, thank you," Elizabeth said. "Do you have a pen in your car?"

Cynthia drove a red 1985 Toyota GT-S with tinted windows. She extended her right arm across Elizabeth's chest and opened her glove box.

"Cynthia!" screamed Elizabeth as the car headed into opposite traffic.

"Found one, Cherie," Cynthia said and corrected her, steering out of oncoming traffic.

"Thank you, but please keep your eyes on the road." Elizabeth noticed the GT-S speed and maneuverability.

Once in the department store, they picked out several dresses for Elizabeth to try on. This was a new Macy's but very busy for a weekday.

While in the dressing room, Elizabeth pulled out the paper and analyzed each part of the message.

"How does the long blue dress fit, Cherie? Do you like it?" Cynthia asked.

"A little too long. Can you find me something similar but not so long?" she requested of Cynthia.

Elizabeth pulled the paper from her purse. She read the word "music box" and knew this was a codeword for radio. She had helped write this kind of messages before while living in the U.K. and working to help the MI5.

The road to Oz is the tickets for the musical Wizard of Oz, and he must be sending a car to pick me up, she thought. *Virltraitor means an American Spy has gone rogue and is hungry for top secret information.*

"I'm back, and do I have some lovely dresses. Not too long but perfect for the theatre experience," Cynthia said, looking through the dressing room door crack.

Elizabeth opened the door and grabbed the dresses.

"Cynthia, let me try on a few of these, and I will be out to show you. Perhaps I might grab some shoes to match one of these dresses," Elizabeth said.

She had tried on the sparkling blue dress, which hugged all of her curves. She admired herself in the mirror. She had gained some weight at her age, but nothing made her feel guilty. Her long blonde hair had grown to the middle of her back, and her green eyes with full lips caused many men to take a second look in passing. She giggled to herself.

The next dress was a floral gown, which made her think of the message again. The plum blossom is the harbinger of spring? Chinese flower and harbinger were words the big galoot asked about.

"What is harbinger?" she questioned and pondered if it was a top-secret file.

"What was that, Elizabeth?" Cynthia asked from the other side of the dressing room door.

"Nothing, just thinking out loud. Sorry," she responded.

She began reading the next part. "0100Z," which means 1 a.m. Zulu time. In New York, that would be a five-hour difference. So, he wants to meet at 8 p.m. in the west section of U. Commit to memory and destroy.

"I think I got it!" Elizabeth said, trying on the newest dress. It was a dark green Rotita shimmering dress with mesh flare sleeves and a v-cut to reveal her tan chest. It also matched her green eyes.

"Perfect, Cherie. Let me see," Cynthia requested.

Elizabeth was impressed with herself and the dress for the meeting. But who could she be meeting? Was this person dangerous? What would happen if this was a prank. She felt immediate stress, and it showed on her face.

"You okay, Cherie?" Cynthia asked. "That dress is amazing. You are going to have so much fun. I am almost jealous."

This elicited a smile from Elizabeth. "Let's find some shoes for my evening gown," Elizabeth said in a British accent.

Cynthia laughed so hard that she began to cry and snorted. This made Elizabeth laugh, and a few women in passing could only stare at both of them, wondering what was so funny.

After laughing and grabbing some lunch, they headed out of the mall, and Elizabeth noticed in the glass of the Hallmark store two black suits following in the distance. To make sure she was correct, she stopped abruptly.

"I miss Carson," she said to Cynthia. "I almost feel guilty going without him."

"Nonsense," Cynthia replied. "I am sure if he loves you as he does, he would want you to enjoy yourself."

"But he is packing, and I am going to the theatre for a major Broadway production," she said, eyeing the glass in the back of Cynthia. The men had stopped and were leaning against a trash can. *So much for being inconspicuous,* she thought.

"And I am sure if he were here watching golf, he would tell you to have a good time with your friend," Cynthia winked and smiled.

"You're probably right." She smiled back, wondering if the two men were FBI or CIA?

Elizabeth fell into silence and slowly strolled. Cynthia was trying to keep pace, but she took longer strides because of her height.

"You okay, Cherie?" she asked. "You in pain at all?"

"No, I feel really good," she said and took off her sling. "Not sure I need this any longer."

She found a trash can nearby and threw the sling in the garbage on the way out the door to the parking lot.

"Well, that was fun, and you're gonna look good, boo-coo," Cynthia lauded.

A cold wind pushed against the glass doors and swept across the lot, sending leaves and another light snow twisting into the sky. Elizabeth could see the men were now close.

"Brrr...Thank you for the sweet comment Cynthia," Elizabeth said.

"Whoops," she said, dropping her shopping bag and leaning to see behind her and Cynthia. The men were still following in the distance.

When they got to the car, Cynthia loaded the bags in and started the car.

"Heat will kick on once we start driving, Cherie," she said.

"Good thing because my butt feels like a popsicle," Elizabeth said, sticking her hands under her legs.

Cynthia pulled out of the parking lot and headed to the freeway. Once on the interstate, she punched the pedal.

"Where are we going now?" Elizabeth asked.

"Back to Estelle's to prepare you for a great night," Cynthia touted. "And away we go."

Cynthia's car sputtered for a moment and revved up, whining as it gained speed.

"Oh boy, here we go again," Elizabeth said, noticing a possible tail from two black Chrysler cars behind them in the side mirror. Whomever they were did a crappy job of staying hidden and were driving on a highway that was still slick with a hint of black ice.

"Peculiar," she said. "I wonder if it was the two from the mall."

"What'd you say, Cherie?" Cynthia asked.

"Do me a favor and get over to the far right when I tell you," Elizabeth said, noticing the lane was clear of other cars. "And slam on the brakes."

"Why?" Cynthia exclaimed.

"Just do it now, please!"

Cynthia ripped the GTS over to the right lane and slammed on the brakes. Smoke billowed up from the highway, and the right wheel cover flew off into traffic. Other cars following from behind slammed on their brakes, and the black Chrysler struck a Mercedes in front of it.

"Oh shit," Elizabeth laughed as she turned to her left to look out the back window. One of the men jumped out of the car and threw his hands up. He looked defeated and stared at the GTS. She recognized the man's face.

"Wilkerson?" she said with a puzzled look on her face. "What is he doing here?"

"Elizabeth, why did you make me do this? We caused an accident. And who is Wilkerson?" Cynthia said, looking out her driver's side mirror.

Elizabeth stared back again at the accident. The Chrysler's front end took the brunt of the damage. Steam was rising into the air from the bent hood. Elizabeth imagined the back end of the Mercedes wasn't much better. An Asian woman driving the Mercedes got out of the car and began to read both men in black suits the riot act.

"No one, Cynthia," Elizabeth sighed. "I am so sorry. I just had a flashback of the bombing."

"Are you all right, girl?" Cynthia said, turning to face her.

"I'm fine," she mumbled. She turned again to look back and noticed one of the suits walking toward them. Elizabeth opened the door, grabbed her purse, walked to the back of the vehicle, and looked at it.

"Nothing wrong I can see here, girl!" she shouted to Cynthia.

"Oh, if you say so," Cynthia said questioningly.

Elizabeth turned to see one of the suits getting closer and holding something that looked like a gun. She heard what sounded like gunfire. She ran to the passenger door and jumped in. But a car passed them, backfiring again with a cloud of black smoke.

"Let's go before the highway patrol shows up."

"Ooh, like the tv show CHiPs?" Cynthia said. "I want to meet that hunk Poncherello or even officer Jon."

"Nope, I don't think he is coming to meet us," she said, looking at Cynthia with a wild smile.

Cynthia pressed the accelerator and her car momentarily stalled, and a yellow golden triangle blinked from the dash. She turned the key again and gave the pedal a more delicate tap and the car jerked back to life and took off. They looked at each other and began to laugh. This was Elizabeth's nervous laugh after realizing they might be in danger. It exhilarated her somewhere in the back of her mind.

If only Carson were here to join in the fun, she thought. She missed him terribly.

CHAPTER 30

The airport train ride to the main terminal was quick and, Carson carried his suitcase to the outside of Chanhi airport to find a taxi to take him to Newton Circus. The dark shadows of the morning were fading and revealed an overcast morning full of grey clouds in the sky, and the air was humid.

Carson flagged down a taxi with *Comfort* written across the door panels. It was a Toyota driven by a large man. The driver jumped out of the car and greeted Carson.

"Good morning, which hotel, sir?" the Singaporean driver asked Carson. He was dressed in a flower-patterned shirt stretched tightly against his large hairy belly exposed just above his khakis.

"I am headed to my condo in Newton Circus, 113 Tan Sim Boh Road, please," Carson announced.

"Sorry, we get many visitors going to a hotel, sir," the driver said and opened the passenger door for Carson, closed it, and put his baggage in the trunk of the Toyota.

The drive to his house was less than 15 minutes. Carson stared out the window, realizing how much he would miss Singapore. Beyond the skyscrapers, heavy traffic, and the bustling crowds, there was a contemporary, cosmopolitan feel to their culture.

"How long have you lived in Singapore, sir?" the driver asked.

Carson looked forward, revived from his trance. He could see the driver's credential and a name with a photo.

"Well, Roy...It is Roy, right?" Carson asked.

"Yes, sir. That is my name. He looked in the rearview mirror at Carson. "How did you...?" Roy stopped mid-sentence, remembering his license with his name and picture clipped to the rearview mirror.

"It has been three years, Roy," Carson replied.

"Do you like living in Newton Circus, sir?" the driver asked.

"It's a busy area and affluent. We are living in a central location with so much to see."

"I have seen almost all of Singapore from the fares I have delivered and the time spent with my family on small short trips," Roy explained.

"How many children do you have there, Roy?" Carson asked.

"We have three girls and one boy," Roy replied. "I have been married 25 years, and our children are very successful. One of my girls is a doctor. The other two are working as accountants. My boy is the youngest and in school. As kids, I took them to the Singapore zoo, gardens, and islands, where we camped."

"My wife and I have a son who is married, and we are about to have our first grandchild. I am excited for him and his wife." Carson thought about how he missed them and could not wait to get back to CONUS.

The driver fell silent, and a heavy surge of rain pelted the roof of the blue taxi. The driver could no longer make out the road and turned on his windshield wipers to the fastest speed. The sound of the rain always seemed to calm Carson, and he returned to his prior initial thoughts of Singapore.

He would miss his walks by Dragonfly Lake, which connects with Marina Bay. Metal sculpted Supertrees that stand 50 meters high act as shade during hot summer days for sightseers walking through the gardens of so many colorful vegetation and palm trees. Singapore is a city with clean streets built around a jungle. And even after spending three years there, there was so much he had not seen.

But he was fortunate to live in the Newton Circus area. Newton Centre is known as a popular eating spot for appetizing hawker food. There are close to 100 stalls serving Hainanese chicken rice, dumplings, lobster, shrimp, fried carrot cake, and Carson's favorite pork rib soup. This was an inexpensive way of picking up a great meal and bringing it home. However, sitting down at a nice restaurant was expensive, and Carson, on special occasions, would take Elizabeth on a date night to an Italian restaurant in the area.

The driver pulled down his visor as the clouds opened up and the blinding sun pierced through a gap.

The driver pulled up to the condominium, got out of his car, popped the trunk to grab his suitcase and opened his door. Carson got out and handed him a $50 bill.

"Thank you, sir. If you ever need a ride in the future, here is my card and number," Roy said.

"You're welcome. Thank you for getting me home safe," Carson said and shook his hand.

For the next 30 minutes, he relaxed and began to unpack his suitcase. The trip was exhausting, and he could hear his stomach growling for food.

On his way to the kitchen, he saw a message on the voicemail of their phone recorder. He pushed the button and listened.

"Mr. Carson, this is World Moving Services. Sir, we want to confirm our arrival on Tuesday, March 5 at 8 a.m. Please call us back at 44-0-21-6597-5443." The machine ended with a long high-pitched beep.

"Okay, I will call them tomorrow. Let's see what's in the fridge," he said to an empty kitchen. He opened the refrigerator and was immediately attacked by a foul odor that made him nearly vomit. The sour milk combined with the mildewed vegetables burned his nostrils.

"If only we hadn't let the maid go before I left..." he said, staring at the picture of Jacob, Janet, and Elizabeth gathered together in the London Eye. The background captures Big Ben and the London Bridge.

His next call was to Elizabeth's cell phone. The ring tone was different, and it kept ringing without an answer. Then, her standard message.

"Whatever recent chain of events led you to leave a message on my voicemail, leave your story here, and I will reach you."

Carson hung up the phone and thought of calling her aunt, but his body reeked of sour milk and underarm odor.

He loved a good long cool shower, and once he dressed in some boxers covered by his robe, he put back on his wedding ring and the engraved watch Elizabeth and Sonya had picked out for his birthday.

In the cabinet, he found some canned soup and crackers. He hadn't cooked in a while, but soup was easy. While the soup cooked on low, he adjusted the rabbit ears on their new television set and found the local news. He stirred the soup and listened to the top news events.

"And by all accounts, Leslie, we believe this was the second major terrorist attack this year by an unidentified assailant," the grey-haired reporter in an overcoat said to the anchor on the split screen. "The explosion sent plumes of black smoke throughout the Fairfax county area and beyond."

Dear God, I think that is Central Intelligence Agency in Langley, Carson thought and tuned back into the TV.

"Traffic is backed up along the turnpike by people who got out of their car to see what had happened. We cannot confirm any injuries or deaths at this time. Reporting for KNBC Washington, I am Greg Curran. Back to you, Leslie."

His thoughts shifted to the attack in New York. Fear swallowed him for a moment realizing Elizabeth could have been killed in the bombing of the tower. Thankfully Jacob alerted him of the event, and some close NY FBI contacts he had made during golf events verified she was safe.

The flight was long, but seeing her brought tears and a broad smile of relief to his eyes. And when he carefully wrapped his arms around her injured body, she told him he felt like a warm blanket of love she had misplaced. She felt like an angel.

"If only I would have stopped her from leaving to go to that radio event," he muttered and threw his fist as if he was punching the air. The disappointment of not being able to protect her after all his military and other training overwhelmed him. His stomach answered back with another rumble.

"Let's see if we can tame you with some Tomato bisque," he replied, rubbing his belly. "Tomorrow, we will head over to Newton Circus to grab something with instant gratification." He set the bowl in front of him on a fold-out tray, sat in his leather recliner, and punched a button on his channel changer to find another station. Channel 12 was televising highlights of the Phoenix Open. After a few moments of eating a few spoonfuls of the soup, he laid back, closed his eyes, thought of his angel, and fell asleep.

CHAPTER 31

E lizabeth began to sweat as the limo pulled up to Estelle's house, and a driver exited the vehicle and opened the back door for her. "Looks like a cruise boat," Estelle said. "Who is this friend you're meeting?"

"I believe she is a scientist," Elizabeth spouted out while looking directly into her eyes. The lie was followed by a smile, and her aunt smiled back.

"Your dress, shoes, and new purse make you look fancy," Cynthia quipped as she stood in the front doorway.

"Thank you, I feel rather special, my dear," Elizabeth said in a cockney accent. The adrenaline pumping through her body was making her feel queasy.

"Have a jolly old time and be safe, please for my sake. I need this job," Cynthia said.

"I second that," Estelle said.

Elizabeth wanted to tell them she was trained to protect herself and that she had packed some unique items in her purse, which also gave her some added advantages. These were CIA weapons given to her by Sonya when she was birdwatching for MI5 or the CIA. The weapon she chose to use to deter someone from attacking her was a pen that sprayed capsaicin or cayenne pepper which would temporarily blind an attacker.

The drive took less than an hour to reach the famed Brooklyn bridge, which they crossed over, and then a few more minutes to arrive at the Shubert theater in the heart of the theater district of Broadway.

"We have arrived, Mrs. Jordon. I do hope the ride was to your satisfaction," he inquired.

"Yes, thank you for getting me here safely."

The driver pulled along the curve, and an usher standing nearby rushed over to open her door, held out a hand, and greeted her.

Elizabeth tipped the driver $40 and asked the usher for directions to the lobby. She was awed by the architecture of the building and overwhelmed by its regality. The front of the building reminded me of her rendezvous point with Sonya in England. The Black Friar pub was frequented by MI5, CIA, and once in a while, a member of the NSU. Everyone with their secrets but posing as everyday blue collar and business cohorts.

Walking through the large double doors through an extravagant lobby, she found a bar and ordered a glass of Chardonnay.

She sipped at the chardonnay and left a lipstick stain on the glass. The nerves in her body were pulsing, and she was trying to keep her hand from shaking. She turned and observed faces in the crowd to see if she recognized anyone. Elizabeth noticed an older gentleman sitting next to her.

"Excuse me, young man could you tell me where the west wing is located?" she asked.

"Princess, I think you may need your eyes checked. I am as old as Moses, but your charm will get you anywhere you like in the Shubert," he replied. "William Garse, pleased to meet you. I, I'm the assist-tant gen gen-eral manager for this p-place."

Garse was in his 80s, portly, with an eagle's nest of hair and thick round glasses. He spoke with a slight stutter, Elizabeth noticed.

"My pleasure as well. My name is Liz. Glad to meet you, William," she said. "Okay, there is some gray in the hair, but you seem young to me," she smiled.

"Oh you...you mean this comb...combover," he laughed. "Some... someone once said grow...grr...growing old is mand...mandatory, but growing up is option...optional. I am just a wise-ass kid inside."

"I will drink to that," Elizabeth said and took a sip of her chardon-nay. "The theater is beautiful, the design in Venetian gold, and the marble floors are stunning."

"Ag...agreed. I am impressed, you know...know your art. As you walk through the am...ambiance will capture you," Garse explained.

"I'm excited to see the rest," she smiled. "My girlfriend wants to meet in the west area. Where is that?"

"Wa...wah...west, huh?" he asked and grinned widely as a Cheshire cat.

Elizabeth showed him the ticket and flipped her hair back with her hand.

"Oh, section U has two seats in the Orchestra area," he said. "That is an odd section, b—but there is mmm...many oddities about this th... theatre."

"You make it sound like an ugly duckling," Elizabeth said.

"No...no odd because there...there is only two...two seats in the sect...section. And the...the view is per...perfect," he explained. "If you have to use the res...restroom, no one to ppp...pass."

"Oh, I see," she said. "Wait, what did you mean about other oddities?"

"Suh...secrets, Liz," he shot back.

"I am good with secrets," she said while putting her finger to pursed lips.

"Okay. Wa...well, if the brass upstairs wants to see what is going on with a pa...pa...production, there's a trap door and a hidden sta...sta... staircase," he revealed.

"That was the real secret, William?" she exclaimed. "Come on, what is the real secret sauce?"

"O...Okay, because you were kind to speak to an old ga...guy like me, I will ta...ta...tell you about the door only a fa...fa...few people know about. A ga...ga...ghost has haunted the th...theater for many ye...years. Spa...spa...specifically the dressing ra...ra...rooms. To escape the theater the...the...owner b...built a connector ta...ta...tunnel to the Broadhurst theatre."

"Nah...ghost stories?" she quipped. "Honestly, William you are a wise-ass."

"Okay, the ghost may be fa...far-fetched. But if you go to the left of the stage to the st...star's dressing a...ra...room there is a door to the back," he said.

"Good secret. I will keep it lock and key," she put the imaginary key to her sealed lips, turned it once, and threw it away.

They both laughed and clinked their glasses together. Garse had a deep laugh like Santa Clause.

"So, now listen to fa...fa...follow the red carpet to...to...the doors heading west." He laughed, pointing in the direction of the auditorium doors.

"Thank you, William. Perhaps I will come back and do a radio show on your ghost," she said.

"Talented and be...beautiful, huh?" he said, looking at his watch. "I have more questions, but I have to get back to my duties. The show must go on."

"Yes, it does," she said, not to his comment but regarding her rendezvous.

"Oh, by the way, if I were 40 years younger, I'd as...ask for your numb...number. You are one gorg...gorgeous wom...woman."

Elizabeth felt her cheeks heating up, and in the bar mirror, she could see herself blushing.

"Yeah, those digits went away when I met the man of my dreams," she said, pointing to the ring on her finger. "He is the only one with those numbers. But thank you for the very nice compliment, William."

Elizabeth grabbed her lipstick-stained wine glass and small purse and followed the golden arrows on the carpet. She noticed the sconces along the green walls and playbills from the former productions and stars to visit the Shubert. The large frames with Sidney Poitier, James Garner, James Earl Jones, Liza Minnelli, and Robert Guillaume all part of productions like *To Kill a Mockingbird*, *Buddy*, *Crazy For You*, *Chicago*, and now *Wizard of Oz*. But she wasn't here for the fanfare, but to find out who was calling.

Elizabeth waited outside the doors for five minutes and then went to section U and sat in seat 104. Next to her, the seat was empty other than a program, which she picked up and opened. When she flipped to the second page, a post-it note was stuck to the page and read, *Look forward and enjoy the show for a few minutes. I will join you momentarily.*

"I am not in Kansas anymore," she whispered.

The lights went down, and the crashing and whooshing sounds began with the start of the production. Just then, a man sat next to her. He was middle-aged with a mustache and brown hair and wearing a tuxedo. Her memory was foggy, but she thought she knew the face.

"Mrs. Osborn, I presume?" he inquired.

"Jesus!" she said in response and stood.

"Don't you mean 'James' or 'honey?'" he replied.

"No, I mean 'James.' What are you doing here? I thought you were dead. I hadn't seen you since the airport when they arrested you."

"Settle down, Beth," he said. "We need to talk. I need your help. So, meet me by the bathrooms in the basement. Okay?"

"Yes," she whispered as a witch screamed and laughed, parading around the stage with her broom.

"Go," he said.

She walked quickly and found the signs to the women's restroom, which was down a flight of stairs. As she marched down the stairs, there was a man leaning against a wall as if he was waiting for his date. She went into the bathroom and washed her hands nervously and paced around until she found the paper dispenser to dry her hands. *Why was Osborn here for her help?* she thought.

Walking out, she noticed the man was no longer standing by the stairs but did notice Osborn was walking down.

"Hey, Beth. My name is Kal Matthews," he whispered, sticking out his hand to hold hers. I don't have much time to tell you this, so listen please. We are both in danger. When we met at the Hong Kong airport, I was on a mission with three other officers. I obtained an electronic file from a Chinese spy helping the U.S. One of our double agents."

"Hold on. Double agents?" she asked. "And you're alive. Where the hell have you been?"

"Dammit, Beth, no more questions. Listen, please," he said.

"Okay, okay."

"Some of these files was downloaded to the Chinese Communist Party. There is a group called the Snow Leopards searching for this file. The leader is calling himself the Chinese Leopard. Agents are dead because this file leaked due to a mole in our government. Thankfully, the CIA has a high-ranking official working with us. As I mentioned, four of us flew into China to meet our contact. The operation Tiger Claw went according to plan until the CCP ambushed us. They killed our contact and shot one of the agents whom we had to leave behind."

He grabbed her hand and started walking up the stairs.

"When I met you at the airport, they hunted me down. You saved my life, and now I get to thank you. However, I slipped the file into your purse in desperation. And we boarded the flight. I stole a purse which looked like yours."

"Except it wasn't, right?"

"For sure. And the next thing you know, I am involved in a black ops mission to Palestine. I was kidnapped, tortured, and a few months ago, released. I have been looking for you, Beth. Where is that purse and the file?"

At the top of the stairway, her hands began to tremble, and she pulled her hand from his. Her small purse nearly fell from her grip.

"Are you the one who attacked me at the World Trade Center?" she scowled.

"What?" he whispered. "What are you talking about? Who attacked you?"

"I don't know. They kept asking me if I had the Harbinger file...."

Matthews' face lost all of its color and he pulled her close.

"Beth, they will do anything to get this file. They have killed multiple agents, and they will kill you. We need to get this to Langley if you know where the file is. Our contact also was able to download information on this file of a CCP project. The file is encrypted, we believe, and it must be highly sensitive because they are killing our agents to find it."

"But I don't have this electronic file," she said. Her pulse was racing. "I don't even remember what purse I was carrying!"

"It's okay, breathe deeply," he whispered.

"What? Breathe deeply? They are hunting us over something you stole, and you want me to breathe deeply? They almost killed me!" She grabbed his lapels with her fists, and her small purse slid down to her elbow.

"What's on the..." she was interrupted by his hand on her head as he thrust her forward and gave her a passionate kiss as two women and a man walked by them. Kal whispered into her ear.

"Meet me back at the seat. We need to keep our cover. We will finish enjoying the rest of the show. Check page 5 of the program. I will leave an address. I need that file, Beth."

Elizabeth was speechless and impressed by the kiss, but scared nonetheless.

"Okay."

Once in their seats, he passed her the program. She looked up to see the beautiful chandeliers, the balcony seats, and the octagonal ceiling paintings. The theatre of 1400 seats was filled for this first performance. As she glanced back to the stage, Dorothy, the Tinman, and the Lion were jumping at the smoke and bursts of fire as she offered the wizard the witch's broomstick. His response was loud, and the whole theatre seemed to shake.

"Not so fast. I have to give the matter some thought. Come back tomorrow," the wizard said.

"I like this part, Kal," she whispered. And looked over to see his head slumped into his chest. She put her hand on his shoulder, and his head fell slightly, revealing he had a hole in his forehead. Elizabeth looked around and into the balconies but saw no one standing.

"Shit. Shit. He's dead!" she tried to scream but was mute. The program fell, and she went to retrieve it, bending over but holding the shoulder of Kal, who slumped slightly forward. The auditorium lights were blinking, and she could not see them in the dark.

"This sucks," she said aloud. And a member of the crowd leaned back to shoosh her. Feeling around the sticky floor, she finally found the program.

"I found it, Kal," she whispered in shock. At that very moment as she began to lean up, she felt a brush of air by her shoulder and heard her dress rip.

"Damn," she whispered again.

She leaned up and turned to look at the left side of her dress and saw a hole in the back of her seat. She was so alarmed that she looked around and up and noticed one of the octagonal panels slowly closing. The realization set in that someone just attempted to assassinate her.

"Are you ready to go home?" the good witch asked Dorothy.

Elizabeth slowly rose and watched as Kal slumped into her armrest. She began to walk briskly, exiting through the auditorium doors into the empty lobby, or so she thought. Leaning against a wall was a skinny young Asian man dressed in a black suit sucking on a lollipop staring intently at her. *The same guy from the stairway*, she thought.

"What are you staring at?" she said, walking in the direction of the restrooms. "You never seen a woman who needs to pee badly?"

She stole a quick glance over her shoulder to see him grinning. He then began running after her.

Elizabeth's quick reflexes kicked in high gear, and she ran for her life.

"Woah," she exclaimed as her high heels caught a roll in the carpet and lost her left pump but kept her balance. She kicked off the right shoe and ran.

It took only seconds, and her pursuer was just behind her. He reached out to grab her leg but missed and face-planted into the carpet. She ran to the rear of the long hallway and noticed a dressing room sign with an arrow pointing right. She slowed and turned the corner when light above her burst, sending sparks and glass into her hair. She covered herself with her arms and fell to a crouching position.

As Elizabeth stood up, she glanced back to see if she was still being chased. The pursuer was still lying on the floor but pointing a gun at her. His second shot whizzed by her but left a hole in her dress and the wall.

"That dress was expensive," she yelled and ran to seek help.

She ran into an actress playing the good witch as she passed the first door. Both women fell to the ground.

"Shit, look out, you crazy bitch!" she screamed.

Elizabeth stood up quickly and looked down the hall. There was the door with a star on it, and she ran towards it.

"I am so sorry!" she called out to the woman.

Once at the door, she turned the knob and slowly entered the disheveled dressing room. Costumes were piled everywhere, along with a rack of dresses that Elizabeth slipped behind. Screams and slamming doors echoed down the hallway. Elizabeth knew the man would eventually find her unless she found the door William had mentioned earlier. She hid behind the dresses and began to shiver from the perspiration and fear.

The door to the room burst open, and the Asian man was on a two-way radio speaking in mandarin. The other voice was screaming at him.

"Don't let that bitch escape," a deep voice said.

"Yes, Xueboa," her pursuer said as he threw aside costumes.

"Hey. Wha...what are you doing?" Elizabeth recognized William's stutter from outside of the dressing room. He was confronting the man digging through costumes.

"Hey, call security!" William yelled down the hall. Startled, the man turned and pointed his gun at William. William began backing up until both were in the hallway.

"He has a gun!" a woman screamed. William screamed at the man, and she could hear them wrestling and bang into the walls. The next sound was the gun firing.

"Aaahh!" William cried, and then a thump hit the ground like a sack of potatoes.

She peeked through the dresses, and between the legs of her pursuer was William's face. William was lying in the doorway in a fetal position holding his chest. She looked into his cold eyes and realized he had left the building. She put her hand over her mouth. People were screaming and running down the hallway.

Elizabeth scooted backwards into a doorknob. In turning the knob, she found a small doorway and pulled on the knob until it popped open, and the stale air brushed her face. She grabbed her purse and slipped through the door and closed it slowly.

"Come on, Liz, you got this," she whispered and heard an echo. A tear was running down her cheek, and she brushed it away. She reached into her purse, fished for her Nokia, and flipped it open. Pushing one of the buttons did not light up the screen.

"Dammit," she said as she stood frozen in complete darkness. Then she remembered her pen given to her by Sonya. When she clicked the end with her thumb, the pen lit up with a dim light.

Crunch. She felt the plastic bottle crush beneath her bare foot. She was thankful it was not glass. She would be extra careful with her next step.

She put the pen down towards her feet and began to walk again. In the distance she heard what sounded like a footstep. She waited in the silence and heard nothing. Perhaps it was her imagination or the phantom step of a ghost. She didn't know whether to laugh or cry. She thought of William's ghost guiding her to safety, smiled, and continued.

CHAPTER 32

Carson wiped his brow; it was a humid morning in Newton Square. A town bell rang 10 times as he stood up from his table at Reagan's Breakfast Shop. The eggs and bacon were exceptional, he thought. He had worked up an appetite since he began to pack at 4 a.m. He completed boxing the kitchenware, the dining room hutch full of Lladró's, and the books in the study, feeling proud he got so much completed.

For the rest of the morning, he would focus on packing Elizabeth's closet, which would take him some time, and then perhaps later in the evening, he would fill his shoes, shirts, pants, and his collection of golf hats. *Oh, and I can't forget my golf clubs in the back storage area.*

Carson entered through the front door of his condo on Tan Sim Boh Road. He remembered the first time laying eyes on this assigned living space the organization picked. The living space was quaint but luxurious inside. The company refurbished the unit. The black and white colonial structure was adapted as a Malay design and elevated to allow airflow underneath to prevent flooding and termites. He would not miss the close quarters of neighbors or the humidity.

Carson checked his watch. It was 11 a.m., and he decided to call Elizabeth. He picked up the phone and dialed Estelle. There was a short series of tones before Estelle answered.

"He-llo," the groggy, monotone voice said.

"Estelle," Carson replied.

"Oh, hey, Carson, how are you, dear?" she asked.

"Still have some jet lag, but doing good," he said. "Is Elizabeth asleep?"

"No, but she is not here either," she replied.

"Where is she?" Carson asked. "How is she feeling?"

"Well, she is feeling better, but you know nothing holds down my niece for long," she answered.

"I also know she has her clumsy spells," he said. "But she is a tough lady. So, to hear she is better and up and doing an activity, I am happy."

Estelle laughed and coughed. "She went with an old girlfriend to see a Broadway play. I believe they were seeing the *Wizard of Oz*."

"That sounds fun. Do you know which girlfriend?"

"Jennifer... Ah, yes, Dr. Jennifer Brown," Estelle remembered.

"Well, at least she is in good hands," Carson snickered.

"She should be home anytime now, and I will tell her you called," Estelle assured him. "How is your packaging going?"

"It's boxing day!" he laughed. "It is coming along. I have to tackle Elizabeth's closet soon and if she doesn't reach me or I don't call, please send a search party!"

Estelle yawned. "Good luck. Well, my dear, I am sleeping out in the living room, waiting for my niece to arrive. I love you, and be careful packing her closet."

"Love you...too," Carson replied as he heard a click on the other end.

He walked into their bedroom, looked at Elizabeth's closet, took a deep breath, and let it out. Some music would be good right now, he thought. He walked over to the stereo and popped in a cassette tape of Alan Jackson and pressed the play button. He started tapping his foot to the lead electric guitar, grabbed a brush on Elizabeth's dresser, and started lip-syncing:

Well, way down yonder on the Chattahoochee, it gets hotter than hoochie coochie. We laid rubber on the Georgia asphalt, we got crazy, but we never got caught.

For a good five minutes he danced and spun an imaginary dance partner. As he sped up the spinning, he felt a bit dizzy and ran into Elizabeth's jewelry box, which exploded when it hit the floor. Jewelry was spread across their marble floor. He noticed a note on the glass door in Elizabeth's handwriting as he picked it up.

Please carefully pack my jewels into the safe. Also, don't forget to pack my purses, and please mark the boxes carefully. Finally, please don't pack my Gucci purse. Bring back on the flight with you.

Which one could be the Gucci? he thought while picking up the drawers and slipping them back in the slots of the beautifully crafted redwood and blue-glass box. Thankfully, the glass had not broken. As he picked up the rings, he noticed one which seemed odd. He had seen this before but had not remembered giving this to her. He put it on his pinky, but it barely fit, and as he maneuvered it with his fingers, a small sharp edge popped up and cut his finger. It was pronged and used to deter or defend against attackers.

"Elizabeth, where did you get this?" he whispered and sucked on the blood spilling from his right index finger.

After getting a Band-Aid on his finger, he finished picking up the jewelry and packed the box carefully with bubble wrap in a box, taped it closed, and marked it as Fragile with a black marker.

He began to pull the purses next and wrap them in brown paper and old newspaper. He never realized how many bags his wife had purchased over the years. Large and small, they had an assortment of colors. One even looked like a tote in light brown with two G's overlapped. He considered for a moment and believed he had found the Gucci bag. He examined the bag and flipped it over, and a square disk fell to the ground and split into two pieces.

For a moment, he considered it might be for her radio scripts, and it had broken during transport. However, as he picked them up and placed the split areas together, both magnetically snapped back together into one disk. A circle of a red raven appeared, and this alarmed Carson.

"Son of a bitch, this is a problem, Lizzy," he mumbled.

He stood up and went into his office, removed their wedding picture from the wall, and slid open a drywall compartment exposing a safe. He used his fingerprint to open the safe and pulled a black folder with the CIA logo.

Inside he found the picture of the symbol of a raven with large, stretched wings. The same symbol is on the disk. As an analyst, he received briefs regularly, but this file was flagged as sensitive compartmented information and an RTOI (Report to Operations Immediately) is recognized.

His first thought was to call his handler, but how would he explain his wife having the file in her purse. He turned it over and examined it. What could be on this disk that made it a top-secret file? He sat down at his desk, turned on his computer, and used NSFNET through the world wide web to ensure encryption standards were met.

He pushed the 3.5 floppy disk into the drive of his laptop and clicked on the file. The file began to download while high-pitched sounds of the internet coming online kept repeating. The file opened, revealing three folders with different three symbol codes. Two of the folders were locked, but one had been left open for viewing.

He opened it, and a list of CIA officers' names appeared. Several of those names had appeared in a recent email as KIA.

"What have you involved yourself in, babe?" he said as he looked at their wedding picture he placed on the desk.

There was a second page that revealed top secret weapons technology. There were detailed engineering drawings circled in red with a note under the picture in mandarin Chinese which he translated. The hair on the back of Carson's neck stood at attention. He knew the Chinese CCP would be looking for this disk.

The internet connected, and, immediately, he wrote an email to the only two people he could trust, Cliff and Sonya. He must get the information out of Singapore safely.

Singapore's Bearcat is naked with blowback COMINT. Rollup in effect.

He directed his cursor and pushed send. A mail symbol started to float across the screen until it disappeared. Carson stared at the green cursor blipping on the black screen background and removed the floppy disk from the drive and disassembled it into two pieces.

He grabbed a copy of Jane Austen's *Pride and Prejudice* from his bookshelf, opened it, and placed one half of the disk into a safe fitted within the book. He put the book into a 12 x 16 envelope and rubber-stamped the front with a P.O. Box address.

As he looked out his small office window, a large orange globe was setting on the horizon, creating shadows of all the large buildings in the distance. He grabbed the envelope and began to head back to the bedroom when the power went out. The computer whined to a stop, and he sat still in the darkness, listening. He could hear footsteps running toward his doorway.

"Shit, here we go," he uttered with anticipation.

CHAPTER 33

Elizabeth walked slowly through the tunnel until she saw a doorway. She pushed the heavy door with her shoulder and burst into a cold, dimly lit alley, nearly falling onto the ground.

"Ow," Elizabeth growled. The pavement was cold and hard on her feet. She clicked the pen, and the survivor light turned off. She put it in her small purse and walked quickly toward the strobing lights on 44th street. Perhaps the limo was still waiting outside the theatre to pick her up, but she wasn't counting on it.

"What's the hurry, girlie?" said a raspy voice in the shadows.

The voice startled Elizabeth, and she froze in place on the balls of her bare cold feet. She scanned both sides of the alley and saw what she thought was a large shadow a few feet away.

"Who are you?" she replied.

"Depends?" the shadow replied.

"Look, creep, I don't have time for this right now," she retorted.

"Lady, I'm no creep or stalker for that matter. I am just a bum down on his luck looking for a light."

A small man stepped out of the shadows and walked towards her. He had long silver hair, a beard, and a short cigar hanging from his mouth. He was dressed in an army green jacket with jeans and cowboy boots. As he stepped closer, the wreak of whiskey followed him.

"I am so sorry, but you startled me," she explained.

"I seem to scare everybody lately. I apologize ma'am," he replied. "Do you happen to have a match or lighter?"

Elizabeth's feet were cold and beginning to ache.

The man looked down at her bare feet.

"Where are your slippers, Dorothy?" he said sarcastically.

"Lost them just outside of Kansas," she whipped. "I was headed to get a taxi to get back."

She looked in her purse, pulled out the pen, and clicked on it twice and a small flame at the tip lit up.

"Wow, now that is cool," he said as he cupped his hands and leaned forward, lighting the cigar. He sucked hard, and a deep red glow lit up the end of the cigar. "Thank you, I appreciate your kindness."

"You're welcome," Elizabeth said.

"You look cold. You want my jacket to warm up?" he asked.

"No. But thank you. How about we make a deal, though?" she suggested.

"What kind a deal, missy?"

"Would you take a $250 for those boots?" Elizabeth asked, holding the money in her hand.

The older man stared at her in disbelief for a moment.

"You serious, missy?"

"You bet. And do me a favor. Take the rest of the money and get yourself a new outfit, shoes, and a warm bed at a hotel. Okay?"

"Deal," he said, pulled off the boots, and handed them to her.

The fit of the boots was surprisingly encouraging to Elizabeth. The smell wouldn't be. *But beggars can't be choosers*, she thought.

"Thank you," she said, handing him the money. "Have a good night."

"You too, ma'am," he said.

She walked to the end of the alley and headed to the front of the Shubert. A dozen NYPD cruisers parked in front of the Shubert and not the limo she hoped would be there. She began searching for a taxi, but several passed her by. Another came towards her, and she waved at the driver.

"Taxi, please?" she pleaded, and he drove past her. As she looked down the street for another, she saw the man who chased her down getting into a vehicle. They were heading in her direction. Panicking, she ran towards the police cruisers when a black van pulled up next to her. The door swung open from the side, and a large black man jumped out and grabbed her from the side and pushed her into the van, and it took off.

"Get off of me! No!" she yelled. Elizabeth kicked and punched back until she felt the pain of a small jolt of electricity through her body that rendered her unconscious.

"She was making you look like a chump there, champ," Wilkerson said.

"Yeah, she's a spitfire and got a nasty elbow," Danielson said as his eye began to swell. "I guess she just needed a little taste of lightning."

"Yeah, next time be careful how long you use that thing. You could have given her a heart attack, and right now, we need her."

"Yeah, well, you got next shift when Xena the Warrior Princess wakes up!" Danielson joked.

"Okay, sunshine. Now can you come up here and join me so we can figure out how to get out of this city?" Wilkerson queried.

Elizabeth could hear the voices in the distance but couldn't make out what was being said. There was so much yelling between the men. She was staring out the frozen window of her dad's station wagon.

"I don't give a flying monkey's shit what you were thinking!" the angry man screamed at her father.

She remembered this trip to the local Piggly Wiggly. Her dad was dropping off a repaired guitar for a friend. A fight broke out, and he threw the case at the man. It knocked him over, and he rolled in the snow to get up and grab grass? No. It was green paper bills scattered all over the ground. Money? Huh? And the sound of a door slamming. Her dream shifted.

The dream moved to a fight with Sonya, who kicked her, knocking her to the ground. Her lesson in Tae kwon do. *Get up, Liz, and fight!*

"What?" Elizabeth screamed, and from a prone position, she jumped up into a fighting stance. Her head was woozy as if she was drunk.

"Hey, jackass, what did you do to me?" she said with a wild look in her eye.

Startled, Wilkerson whipped the vehicle left and right, and Elizabeth lost her balance and slammed into the side of the van. Her heart raced, and she sat for a moment to catch her breath.

"HOLY SHIT!" Danielson said as Wilkerson got control of the vehicle and exited off an interstate ramp and came to a red light at the bottom.

"Jesus, Elizabeth, it's okay, settle down," Wilkerson said and pumped on the brakes to slow down.

"Wilkerson?" she said, perplexed. "What are you doing here?"

"Nice to see you too, Elizabeth," he replied.

"But how could you—"

"—know how to find you?" he finished her sentence. "Surveillance and intelligence. Part of my job at the CIA."

"Again, why are you here?" she asked.

"Director wants you back at Langley. He considers you an asset and a target," Wilkerson responded.

"Get down!" Danielson drew his 9MM and pointed it at Elizabeth.

"Jeez, Danielson, bring it down a notch." Wilkerson turned to him and gestured to lower the weapon. Elizabeth complied and dropped to her knees, and several gunshots blew out the back window as a black Mercedes sped towards the van.

Blood sprayed the front windshield as Danielson's head exploded from the impact of one of the bullets.

"Oh my god!" Elizabeth screamed.

Wilkerson pressed the accelerator and started speeding up the turnpike to outrun the Mercedes.

Wilkerson looked in his rearview mirror as the headlights edged closer.

"Stay down, Jordon, and hold onto something!" Wilkerson shouted. Several bullets ripped through the top side of the van. The Mercedes then pulled to the driver's side and slammed into the side. Elizabeth rolled across the van's floor, and Danielson's body flopped side to side.

Wilkerson drew his revolver, leaned around his seat, and fired several rounds at the men in the Mercedes. It ran into the side of the median and slowed for a moment, then launched toward them.

"Elizabeth, we're coming up on water, and I am going to dive. Get to the back and open the doors. Before we hit the water, you need to find something to hang onto, okay?" Wilkerson explained.

She was silent, and she could hear the Mercedes accelerating.

"Yeah!" she screamed.

Wilkerson jerked the van right into the aluminum railing and sent the van over the side of the small bridge.

"Father, forgive me for my sins. Please take care of my son, Jacob, his wife, and our grandbaby. I love you, Carson," she said as the water crushed the van.

Elizabeth grabbed a handle on the side door. The impact of the van hitting the water sounded and felt like the bomb that went off at the World Trade Center. She floated with one hand in the air for a moment and then was slammed to the side wall.

"Oof," the impact knocked the air out of her, and she struggled to breathe for a moment.

Slowly the van filled with cold, frigid water and Elizabeth let go and started swimming out of the van toward the surface. She looked back to see the van disappearing into the blackness. She did not see Wilkerson but kicked her way to the surface for air.

The Mercedes slammed on its brakes, and several men got out.

"What a crazy son of a bitch!" one said.

"If they're alive, we will find them. Spread out!"

Elizabeth sucked in a deep breath and submerged her head under the water. She began to swim until she found a shoreline and crawled into some heavy brush and sat for a moment. She was breathing hard and was shivering. She emptied her boots and ripped part of her torn dress. She had to keep moving up the embankment and stay warm. As she slowly crawled and made her way to the top, she peeked over and saw no one around.

"Go," she willed herself to walk briskly.

The sun was beginning to rise, and she could see a donut shop a few blocks away. She rushed to get there. Perhaps they would allow her to use a phone to call Estelle.

Elizabeth could barely push the door open. She was shivering and fell onto the floor of the shop. Both the owner and a server making coffee rushed to pick her up.

"Ca-ca-can you please help me?" she asked. "N-need a phone," she quivered.

"Please sit down, ma'am. Let's get you some hot cocoa," the owner said. "We'll call the police."

"Na...na...no. Just n-n-need to warm up and call my aunt, please," Elizabeth begged.

The owner rushed into the back of the store. He kept a cot and blanket for late nights. He grabbed the blanket and put it around Elizabeth. And the server brought her some cocoa. She shook violently and sipped at the hot beverage for several minutes until she felt warm again.

"What happened to you?" the owner said, sitting in front of her.

"I got drunk and walked home and fell into the river," Elizabeth told the owner. She felt terrible having to lie, but it was better than the truth.

"Okay, let me go get the phone," he said. "By the way, I'm Mitch. I am glad you're okay. Do you want a donut on the house?"

"Thank you for your kindness. I will just pay for it after my call," Elizabeth said. And then she realized she did not have her purse or her dead phone. But she was alive. Mitch came back and presented her with a jelly donut and the phone.

"Hello," Estelle yawned.

"It's me, Auntie. I need you to come and get me."

CHAPTER 34

C arson looked at his wristwatch illuminated in green. His cover was blown, and he expected uninvited guests soon. He dressed in blue jeans, a brown shirt covered by a button-down, and lightweight combat boots.

His go-bag was set in the closet and prepped with a first aid kit, set of clothes, guns, ammo, flint, flashlight, rations, and two fake passports, all sealed in plastic. He placed the disk in the front of his bag and then packed one legal envelope with a stamped address.

He shredded and burned all classified files in the safe and lit candles in each room. He grabbed his wedding photo to put in his bag.

"In the fight of my life here, Liz," he said, looking at the picture. "But a little bit of bleach and sugar should do the trick, and if I don't make it...well...I love you."

A knock came at the door. He said nothing. Then some pounding. And finally, with no answer, the door was kicked in and splintered the frame. Three men in black with flashlights rushed down the hall.

He surmised that taking on three men was not wise, so he waited behind the laundry door. They stopped near him and the kitchen.

"Split up. Mr. T said to trash this place until we find it," the leader directed to his crew. They wore black balaclava masks, army boots, and assault rifles.

The leader was smaller and stockier than his counterparts. He headed for the kitchen, while the other two began searching the bed-rooms. Carson shadowed the leader.

Wonder if this Mr. T is the notorious gangster of Singapore? Carson thought. He was a murderer, drug trafficker, pimp, and thief. Carson had seen a few pictures of him in his CIA brief before coming to Singapore. The man was 5'11, black hair, lean, and known for his patterned shirts and smoking a cigar. For years, authorities believed he fled to another country with rewards posted for his arrest. His people were tactically trained.

The condo was extremely dark, and Carson could see the light in the kitchen. He peered around a corner to see the leader standing in front of the refrigerator. All the cabinets were open, and a box full of Tupperware was scattered all over the floor. He quietly approached the man.

"I assure you there is nothing in the freezer," Carson said with a whisper.

The assailant whipped around, looking startled, and met the iron on his jaw. His eyes rolled in his head and flopped on the floor. Carson closed the freezer door and heard one of the men approaching quickly from the back bedroom. Carson greeted him in the dining room.

"Can I offer you some coffee?" he said as they stood nearly toe-to-toe. This attacker was much bigger and swung his fist into Carson's solar plexus. The blow made him double over trying to breathe. The club dropped to the floor, and the attacker kicked him in the face. Both hurt Carson, but he rolled backward and lifted himself, ready to fight.

"That was not hospitable at all, hoss," Carson quipped and lifted his cupped hand and motioned the man to come at him.

The large man grunted, smiled, and rushed towards Carson with a large bowie knife. The man swung the blade, and Carson side-stepped and whipped one of his legs, tripping the large man who crashed head first into the granite kitchen island. The man was out, and blood spilled all over the marble floor.

The third intruder, who must have heard the commotion, came up from behind and tackled Carson onto the floor. Carson rolled him over back and forth in the blood of the other man. Finally, Carson was able to gain control of a wrist with his other hand, grabbed a handful of hair and mask, and tugged it off.

"Lan jiao!" his attacker screamed. Carson, who was on top of him, punched him in the mouth and noticed a large scar which stretched across his lips.

"I think you meant to call me a dickhead, partner, not a penis bird," Carson said sarcastically.

The scarred attacker turned red, punched wildly, caught Carson in the chin and sent him backward. The man pulled out his Glock, tried to stand, but slipped in the blood. He fired off four shots that missed Carson and wounded their leather sofa. Carson jumped up and ran towards the bedroom, and his attacker tried to follow but kept slipping.

Carson shut the bedroom door and pushed a dresser to block the entrance. Then he placed the lit candle on the dresser and grabbed his go-bag. Shots pierced the bedroom door as Carson scurried to the back of the closet. He heard a grunt from the attacker trying to push the bedroom door open.

Ka-boom! The dresser hit the floor, and the candle hit the floor, igniting a purplish flame that engulfed his attacker and the rest of the condo.

"Ahhh, you bastard!" the attacker screamed.

Carson opened a trap door and escaped by jumping down into the mud beneath the condo.

He began crawling in the dark until he reached an embankment with a tree line.

Sirens wailed as fire engines approached the neighborhood. Carson was camouflaged by the jungle and watched as the flames raged through the condo. He hoped no innocents were harmed. He hurt everywhere on his body, and his clothes was caked in blood, mud, and sweat.

An explosion inside the house sent red embers into the sky. Carson would remember the smell of sadness burning away their memories. He took a long pause of reflection. I need to get to Sacred Heart Parish, he thought.

Carson was a practicing Catholic with a heavy heart of guilt and spent each day praying and each week at the confessional. The parish was only a mile from his house, but it would serve as a safehouse for now. He would have to travel incognito outside the normal streets without lighting.

Before leaving, though, he had one more important item to complete. He dug into his bag and fished out his Globalstar satellite phone and his glasses and called the only person he could trust.

"Hello?" Sonya said.

"White Russian, this is Bearcat," he said. "I have become naked."

"Stay out of the cold and find your safe spot?" she said.

"Time is my enemy," he responded. "And not sure if my controller can be trusted with a hot package. I need a good brush."

"I see. Your timepiece is a friend. Do you remember what I showed you?"

"Roger," he replied and turned the bezel on the watch. The green illumination became red as he triggered the locating signal. His adrenaline peaked and his body hurt, but he knew he had to press on. Soon Sonya would be coming to meet, and he would handoff the Harbinger file. He put on his night vision glasses and walked down an empty street.

CHAPTER 35

"Sweetheart...wake up," Janet said with a whisper in her husband's ear. He responded with a loud snort and snore.

"Jesus, Mary, and Joseph, will you wake up!" Janet screamed. "Jacob, I am having this baby. My water just broke."

Jacob jumped out of bed like he was thrown into an ice-cold lake.

"You're...having the baby. Okay! I got everything ready!" he screamed with excitement.

"Do you have the stuff I asked for?" she asked.

"Suitcase with the gown, slippers, bathrobe, diapers, toothbrush, toilet paper, baby seat," he said. "Check and mate."

"Okay, okay," she laughed. "Aaaah, hmmm. I'm having another contraction."

Jacob steadied his wife by holding her arm and sat her on a rocking chair near their bed.

"All right, stay here, and I will go put everything in the car for the third and last time, I hope," he said and grabbed the bag.

Janet was a week overdue, and her doctor planned to do a C-section if another week passed.

"Hey, my bundle of joy, it's time to meet the world this morning," she said, massaging her belly.

Jacob ran into the room with the keys in his hands. "Let's go, darling. Let me help you."

"Are you forgetting something, babe?" she asked with a wince.

"Noooo. I don't think so," he responded.

"Put some damn pants on over those boxers," she cried in pain. "I'm sure no one wants to meet Captain Love Staff."

"Oh yeah," he said, looking down.

Once in their 4-Runner, it took 10 minutes to get to Christ Hospital in the heart of Cincinnati. He pulled up to the emergency room doors and ran inside.

"Can you help me please? My wife is having our baby," he said with a raised voice to a nurse sitting at a desk.

"How far along?" she said with a drab voice.

"She's overdue by a week," he answered.

"Let's go," she said and followed with a wheelchair.

Once inside and prepped, the nurse checked her progress.

"Lucky eight," she smiled at Janet. "You are dilated 8 centimeters and nearly ready. Let's get you on your side."

"What else does she need?" Jacob asked.

"A little pain relief," the nurse responded, holding a needle in her hand. "A little epidural in her lower back will help."

Jacob decided to leave for a moment to call both sets of grandparents. He kissed his wife on the forehead.

"I'll be back in five minutes. I have to grab a payphone and call your mom and mine," he said.

"Get back here pronto," she cried, and a tear made its way down her cheek. "I can't do this without my partner."

Jacob ran down the hallway and realized he had no quarters. *I will have to make a collect call to Aunt Estelle's house and then to Janet's mom, Mrs. Drury,* he thought. He waved down a nurse walking toward him.

"Can you tell me where I can get change to make a phone call?" he asked.

"Follow this hallway to the end, turn right, and there is a break room with a candy machine. I believe they have one of those coin machines there," she said, pointing her finger straight ahead.

After grabbing a few crumbled dollars in his jeans, he cashed them in for some quarters and dropped them into the hospital vending machines for a soft drink and candy. Jacob looked at his watch.

"Quarter to seven," he said aloud.

"What?" A man making a call turned and looked at him.

"Whoops. Sorry," he responded sheepishly. "Hey, what do you know? I got a quarter to call my mom and tell her the good news. We're having a baby. I mean, my wife and I are having a baby."

"Congrats," said the man holding the receiver to his ear and staring oddly at Jacob. "Good for you, buddy."

Jacob hesitated before he dialed Janet's mother. Teresa Drury was not fond of Jacob marrying her daughter because of the class disparity. The Drurys lived in Terrace Park, and the Jordons were considered middle-class gypsies traveling Europe. Once their daughter became pregnant, both Edwin and Teresa accepted Jacob.

"Hello, Mrs. Drury?" he said.

"Who is this?" she said sternly. "Don't you telemarketers ever quit. It's early morning, for Christ's sake."

"No. It's Jacob, ma'am," he replied. "We're having the baby."

"Holy shit!" she yelled. "Edwin, get up! We have to go to the hospital. Our baby is having a baby."

"Okay, see you in a few minutes at Christ Hospital," he said and heard a dial tone.

Jacob pushed a few more quarters in the phone and dialed his Great Aunt Estelle. Several rings passed before getting her voicemail.

"It's Jacob. We are having a baby. Tell my mom to call Christ Hospital. We will be in room 146," he said and hung up the phone.

He knew the next call would be much more money, so he made a collect call to his dad. He dialed zero and waited for the operator.

"I'd like to make a collect call to Singapore, please," he said, giving her the number.

"One moment, please," she said, connecting the call.

The phone rang, and then an automated voice in a British accent announced, "This phone is no longer in service...the number you dialed is no longer in service." The phone call ended.

The operator was still on the line holding. "Is there another number we can dial, sir?" she asked.

"No, thank you very much," Jacob said, bewildered and hung up the phone. Why would his dad cancel the phone service now? *The movers aren't due to be there yet*, he thought.

He walked back to Janet's room, and nurses were scrambling in and out. He stopped a nurse passing by him.

"Can you tell me what is happening, please?" Jacob asked.

"Are you Mr. Jordon?" she asked.

"Yes. Are my wife and baby okay?" he asked.

"We have been looking for you, sir," she said. "We are just taking precautions after her blood pressure dropped. The doctor has asked you to wait in the lobby for the moment."

"That's my wife in there, and I don't want to leave her when she needs me!" he screamed.

"I promise we are taking care of her. But we need also to protect your baby. As soon as they are both stable, we will come and get you, okay?" the nurse responded sweetly. "You are a good husband and about to become a great father, and we just want to treat mama right now, so there are no complications."

"I want to be there during our child's birth," he said.

"You will, but let us do our job," she said as she walked with him to a small waiting room with a tv and some vending machines.

"Thank you. Please take care of her," he said with trepidation.

CHAPTER 36

Carson pulled the hood over his head and walked briskly through the dark streets. He crossed lanes, zig-zagged between cars looking in the rearview mirrors to see if he had a shadow in the distance. He was sure Chinese surveillance was on the lookout.

He approached Sacred Heart from the back. Carson entered the parsonage attached to the church to search for Father Joseph Linly and knew precisely where to find him.

"Boy, those chocolate chip cookies smell amazing," Carson complimented.

"My boy, they consume me more than I wish I could consume them," he replied.

"Joe, your belly begs to disagree," he chuckled, and they both laughed and hugged.

"You look worse for wear, my son. What happened?"

"Perhaps I can provide my sacrament of penance?" Joe replied.

"Follow me," Joe said, and they headed into the nave and found a confessional.

"Bless me, father, for I have sinned." Carson crossed with his left hand, which felt awkward. "Father, I am in trouble, and I need to stay out of sight."

"I am not sure I understand, but I will do everything to help," he said.

He confessed his sins to the priest and provided vague details of why he ran and hid. Many parishioners adored Father Linly, or just Joe. He was the Pastor. Carson had created a bond with the priest. They played pool, golf, and cards together. Carson also dedicated time teaching Sunday school.

"Carson, pray with me and then meet me in the kitchen for a cookie," he said. Joe led Carson to the kitchen, grabbed two cookies, and opened a door that blasted both of them with a stale scent of wine. They headed down wooden stairs into a basement that looked like a Mobile Army Hospital Unit.

"Now, let's get you patched up," he said.

"Uh, okay? What is this place?" Carson asked.

"Well, my son, this has been here for some time, and we provide health care to the needy. Sometimes it's battered wives, or the poor, or terminal prisoners," he said. "Of course, we also go to the prison to treat injured prisoners."

"But I didn't realize you were a medicine man," he said sarcastically.

"I was a doctor before I became a priest, Carson. I served in the Foreign Legion as a medic in Cambodia. Our doctor was killed during an exercise, and I was promoted," Joe explained.

"And here I thought I knew you," he retorted.

"Oh, that's ripe coming from the undercover agent posing as a golf engineer," Joe said.

"Hey, that was part of my confession," he replied.

"In God's confidence, the sacramental seal is inviolable," Joe said. "Besides, it's not every day I meet a real CIA agent."

"By the way, the cookie tastes as good as it smells but needs a chase of milk," Carson sniped.

"Well, I can't offer any milk, but perhaps some wine may imbue your palate," Joe said.

Joe uncorked a bottle of Chateau Angelus and handed it to Carson, who drank half of the bottle. Joe noticed Carson looked pale and was bleeding from his left shoulder.

"Carson, let's look at your shoulder," Joe said.

Carson pulled off his bloody brown shirt. There was a large bullet hole in his shoulder that was bleeding profusely.

"We need to get that bullet out of your shoulder and patch it up. Keep sipping on that bottle while I get some clean instruments to work with," he said.

Carson finished the wine with a few swigs of the bottle. He was feeling tired after putting in a good fight.

Joe entered the room with another bottle and a thermometer. Carson was getting worse faster than expected, and his temperature read 103 degrees.

"Carson, you're running a high fever. I have to cut out that bullet, and it's going to hurt." Joe handed him another bottle. "Whiskey?"

Carson took a swig and motioned for him to begin. Joe laid Carson back on the gurney and inserted an IV into his arm. He sterilized the scalpel in alcohol and began to cut into the wound. The pain was so excruciating that Carson blacked out.

He dreamed of being on a beach alone with Elizabeth. The sound of light wind blowing the palm trees above them and the ocean waves crashing onto the beach and rolling up to their feet. This was a halcyon moment for Carson. He leaned over and kissed Elizabeth. The kiss was tender and sensual.

"How do you feel about pecan pie and wine?" he asked Elizabeth.

"Wine?" she asked.

"Georgia. That's my next assignment," he said. "Did you know Georgia is the birthplace of wine?"

"No. I hate pecans, and wine makes me sick," she said with a stern look. "No. Not this time. Please help me, God."

The wind kicked up, and the skies turned black. The ocean turned red, and lightning streaked across the sky. The trees above began to bend, and Carson and Elizabeth began to run into a jungle he did not recognize. It began to rain hard, and Carson could no longer see Elizabeth but heard her cries for help.

"Elizabeth? Elizabeth, where are you?" he yelled in his sleep.

A bright light then surrounded his body and felt warm, secure, and serene. He felt washed of all of his guilt and insecurities. He was confident and strong, and he felt no pain. The light became brighter, and he felt a presence pushing him, and he closed his eyes. When he opened them, the stench of wine permeated his nostrils.

"Welcome back, Carson," Joe said.

"What?" Carson said. "How long was I…"

"Asleep?" Joe said. "For the past two days."

"And the bullet?" he queried.

"I got it out cleanly, but we need to ensure no nerves were damaged," Joe said.

Carson leaned up and propped himself with his left elbow, and Joe helped him to a sitting position.

"Are you hungry?" Joe asked.

"Starved," Carson admitted. "Cookies again?"

"Good thing you haven't lost your sense of humor," Joe smiled. "No, the parish sisters made a full meal this morning. Eggs, bacon, and a waffle."

"This is better than a hotel," Carson said.

"Well, don't get comfortable yet," Joe said. "There is a table and chair I have set up for you. Let's walk over and sit you down."

"With pleasure," he said.

Once seated, Joe placed the local newspaper on the table and slid it over to Carson. The headline read:

Singapore Manhunt for Alleged American Killer

There was a picture from his entrance into customs used in the paper. The black and white image was unrecognizable.

According to the article, the fire burned everything inside the condo, and the police found a deceased male—a local Singaporean with a criminal background. The SPF informed the press that anyone who comes in contact with Mr. Jordon should call the police right away, for he is considered armed and dangerous.

"I have to leave, Father," Carson said. "The church has been good to our family, but I will not drag you into this nonsense."

"Too late," Joe retorted. "You are a member of this parish, and I know the truth. That's enough for me. Let's get you back home to Elizabeth."

"Really, Father, you have done more than enough," Carson insisted.

"Carson, I am glad to help and have an idea," Joe said. "If we could get you to Junk Island, it's abandoned. And then you can coordinate a pickup."

"That may work," Carson said as he collected his thoughts.

"I will leave you to your thoughts," Joe said as he walked up the stairs. "I'll bring you breakfast momentarily."

As Joe entered the kitchen, one of the head nuns came to see him.

"Father Linly, a Singapore police officer and superintendent are in the main rectory waiting to speak with you."

"Tell the police I will be up in a jiffy. Need to put on my collar," he said.

The two officers greeted Father Linly when he entered the room. He immediately recognized one of the men who did attend church frequently.

"Father, I am Superintendent Tam Hok Joe, and this is officer Ben Ho Chin," Joe said.

"Tam, how are you?" Joe said. "It has been a while since I have seen you in church."

"Ah...yes, Father," he blushed. "Long, thankless hours in this job sometimes, plus weekend duty."

"Oh, I understand, Tam," Joe said. "Are you here for confession today, or is there something else I can help with, officers?"

"Father, we are looking for one of your parishioners, Carson Jordon," Tam said and pulled out a pack of American Indian cigarettes. "You mind if I smoke?"

"No, but let's take a walk out of the rectory," Joe said as he led them away towards the kitchen.

"What has Mr. Jordon done exactly?" Joe asked.

Tam leaned over and lit his cigarette with a match. "You haven't seen the news, Father?" he asked.

"No, I can't say I am up to speed with current events," he replied.

"Mr. Jordon is wanted for questioning after a Singapore resident was found burned to death in his condo," he said, exhaling a large breath of smoke.

Carson could hear heavy footsteps above him. The dust from the floorboards seeped into the air. He could listen to Father Joe speaking with a gruff Singaporean.

"Well, I am sorry to hear about the local who perished. Do you know his identity yet?" he asked.

"I'm afraid I can't share that information with you, Father," Tam said.

"Oh, yes, I imagine that is part of your investigation," Joe said.

"He was the son of the Chinese consulate and a local gang member," officer Joe said. "And Chinese officials have asked us to turn over Mr. Jordon for criminal espionage."

Tam nearly inhaled his cigarette. He shot an unapproving glance at officer Joe and then met the priest's eyes.

"When was the last time you saw Mr. Jordon?" Tam asked.

"Not long ago to renew his rights of the sacrament," Joe said.

A tiny nun approached with urgency.

"Father, his excellency is on the phone asking for you," a young Singaporean nun said.

"Yes, tell him I will be there momentarily," he instructed.

"Yes, Father."

"Gentleman. I do apologize, but my duty calls," Joe said.

"Father, if you contact Mr. Jordon, please call us immediately. He is armed and considered dangerous."

"I shall reach out to you," he said. "Here now, let me show you out, gentlemen."

The footsteps left the kitchen, and Carson had gathered from the conversation that the local police were looking for him, and he must leave soon. He was weak, but he stood up from his seat and grabbed his pack. As he zipped it open, the satellite phone lit up, but he did not recognize the number. He answered.

"You have what I want, Mr. Jordon," the deep disguised voice said. "I can pay you handsomely."

"That is not happening, and this is a secure government line which can be traced," Carson said.

"Mr. Jordon, don't insult me," the voice grew angry. "You can run, but you won't get far, and I'm giving you one chance to accept my offer."

"Like I said, that is not happening," Carson said, and the phone call ended with three beeps. Carson knew this was not local but international.

CHAPTER 37

The phone kept ringing at Jacob's great aunt's house. It was not like Estelle to not answer.

"Where could everyone be today?" Jacob whispered into the phone.

"He-ll-o," Estelle said, out of breath.

"Auntie, it's Jacob. Is mom there, please?" he asked.

"Is everything okay, Jake?" she said.

"Yes and no. Janet is having the baby, but there is something wrong with her blood pressure," he told Estelle.

"Okay, here is your mom," she said and handed the phone to Elizabeth.

"It's happening?" Elizabeth asked. "How many centimeters is she dilated, son?"

"Nine centimeters," he responded. "But, Mom, something is wrong with Janet, and they are not giving me much information."

"What have they told you so far?" she asked.

"She has higher blood pressure than normal, is all I know," he said. "It's called preeclampsia."

"Sweetheart, I am sure the doctor will take care of her," she said. "I wish I could be there for both of you."

"Mom, I am worried about Janet," he said as his voice cracked, and he felt a tear roll down his face. He looked down the hall and noticed a doctor and nurse walking in his direction.

"The doctor is coming, Mom, and I want to speak with him, so I am going to call you back later. Okay?" he said.

Elizabeth was so tired and shaken from the events of the night before that she could only stare into space. Estelle pushed her shoulder.

"Yes. Yes, darling. Sorry. Let me know as soon as possible," she said and hung up the phone.

"Mr. Jordon. I am Dr. Alexander Gillette. We met a few months ago during Janet's prenatal care check-up," he said.

"Yes, doctor, I remember, thank you," Jacob said.

"So, I don't want to alarm you, but Janet will not have a vaginal birth. We will prep her for surgery to perform a C-section," he said. "Because of the abnormal blood pressure, we want to make sure both Janet and your baby are safe. Do you understand?" he asked.

"So, can I be in the room with my wife?" he asked. "And will she be awake?"

"Yes to both questions. We wanted to come down and get you prepared as well," he said. "If there are any concerns during the procedure, we will escort you out of the delivery room. But this should go smoothly."

CHAPTER 38

After breakfast, Joe led Carson with his go-bag to the shower, gave him a towel, and fetched him a new pair of jeans and a brown T-shirt.

"I hope these fit. I spoke with a parishioner who ran our food and clothing pantry and gave her a general description of the sizes I needed," Joe said.

"Thank you, Father. All I need now is a plane ticket and a cold beer," he joked.

"Got you covered on the beer, but not the ticket," he said. "Once you're done with the shower and dressed, maybe I can help you get some transportation."

"Thank you again," Carson said as he closed the door and turned on the shower. He rummaged through his pockets and pulled out a small pen knife, a key, and the disk. The disk was split into two pieces for security. One half he would have to send to Langley. The other half would remain in his possession until he could connect them and share the top-secret information with a high-ranking official.

"Carson?" Joe said with a knock at the door.

Carson opened the door, and Joe thrust a Budweiser through the opening.

"Thanks," he laughed and closed the door.

The hot water was refreshing, and he imbibed the cold can of beer. Both were exhilarating. He rinsed off the caked blood all over his body and watched as the cascade of red water ran down his legs and feet into the drain. He ran water over his wounds and was thankful he survived the battle royale with the three thugs.

After showering, he brushed his teeth and then went through the contents again of his go-bag. His 1911 with three rounds of ammo, five flash grenades, bowie knives with compass, first aid kits, flashlights, glow sticks, and a canteen with water and protein rations. The envelope he would give to Joe to mail at a later date.

Joe was sitting on of the gurneys when Carson entered the room. He had a map he laid out and a plan to help Carson in his escape from Singapore.

"Carson, the SPF was here today asking questions about you. The main streets, railways, and harbor ways are locked down by the police," Joe explained.

"Can you get me transport towards the bridge of Johor?" he asked.

"Carson, did Jesus feed multitudes of people with seven loaves and a few fish?" Joe jested.

"He did," Carson smiled. "Can you do one final thing for me, Father, please?"

"What's that, Carson?" Joe asked.

"I have a book that needs to be mailed to a friend," he said with a wink. "Can you please send this indiscriminately?"

"You can count on me, Carson."

"Thank you for everything, Father," Carson said. "I guess I owe you a free round of golf soon."

As they laughed, there was commotion above them, and one of the sisters was yelling loudly. Joe waved at Carson to grab his pack and the map. Joe led him down a hall.

"There is a door at the end on the left. Outside is a truck filled with vegetables covered by a tarp. Good luck, son, and please be careful. May God be with you." Joe hugged him.

CHAPTER 39

The old truck putted down the street with a few backfires, making Carson jump once or twice during the trip. He laid in the bed of the truck, which was covered by a tarp. He laid prone behind the loaded vegetables. The onions were pungent and tried not to sneeze when they came to a stop at intersections.

Carson's goal was to make it to the next church and then hide until nightfall when the roads would be easier to maneuver undetected. The truck came to a hard stop, and he rolled back into the cab.

"Please roll down your window, sister," a stern voice said.

"Yes, of course!" she yelled loudly through the glass. The window began to squeak as she turned the knob and would only lower a few inches.

"We are required to see the back of the truck, sister," the voice said. Carson gathered that his must be the SPF.

"May I ask why you want to look at my vegetables and beef, officer?" she asked.

"We are looking for this man. Have you seen him?" he asked.

"Oh yes, Carson Jordon. What a very kind man. He goes to our church and helps on our staff," she said.

"Well, he is wanted for questioning in a murder investigation," the SPF officer replied.

"Well, I have not seen him, and this load of food is going to the orphanage to feed hungry children. I have to be there in the next 15 minutes so we can start preparing food for dinner later tonight," she told the officer.

"Well, I still have to look, sister," he said.

"Officer, do you have to take off the whole tarp? It took me forever to tie this down, and I need to hurry," she said.

"Okay, okay," he said. "Let me take a quick peek underneath." The officer looked quickly underneath only to see bananas, onions, a large leafy vegetable, and a large cut of beef.

Carson's heart felt like it may come out of his chest, and he was sweating profusely from the humidity. He hid behind the leafy vegetables and the beef and thanked the Lord he did not have to confront the local police.

"Thank you, sister, you can move along," he said.

The sister put the truck in gear and began moving again at a slow pace, but Carson was thankful to have a flow of air coming into the truck's bed. As they turned down a quiet street, the road became extremely bumpy, and the truck backfired again. This time, though, it stopped, and Carson wondered if the nun had come to another checkpoint. The front door opened and closed, and he could hear footsteps.

"Oh, dear," she said and unhooked the tie down on the tarp. "Mr. Jordon, we have a flat, and I don't have a spare tire. I had to leave it behind to make room for you and the food. We have to get you somewhere safe while I call someone back at the church to come out and change it for us."

"Sister, Sacred Heart has done enough. Bless you," he said and put his bag on his back and a hat and sunglasses. He would head through Chestnut Nature Park to avoid detection and, especially, capture.

* * *

"Good afternoon, sir," Mr. G said to the Snow Leopard commander.

"Pissed! I paid you a lot of money, Guy, to do one thing, and you failed!" the commander screamed.

"Commander, take it easy. My gang runs this city, and we will find him. I own the damn SPF. He killed one of my best members, and I intend to repay the favor," Mr. G replied.

"Listen, you little pill pusher, do not kill him!" the commander warned him. "Hurt him, yes. But he is mine, and he has the information I want. So don't cut his tongue out as you have in the past. This is my kill!"

Mr. G. had met the commander they called the Snow Leopard just once in Jakarta as enemies. Both were searching for a Thai national who stole a blue diamond from the Arabs. The leopard commandos were dangerous and nefarious.

The commander cut a deal with Mr. G after a jungle battle, and the Singapore gang surrendered. The contract was to locate the thief and the diamond, and they would not kill his crew and burn their bodies. In the end, Mr. G was paid handsomely. While Mr. G was known to be ruthless in Singapore, he was nothing like this psychopath. Once the thief was captured, they branded his forehead and cut him with a small scalpel. Some cuts were so severe that blood rained from the ceiling. Mr. G decided his corpse would never bear the brand of the claw.

"I will punish him, but nothing more," Mr. G recoiled.

"My team has tracked the American just east of the Singapore zoo. Here are the coordinates: 1°27'04.7»N 103°46'09.3," the commander said. "Find him, capture him, and I will transfer the $500,000 reward to your Swiss account."

* * *

Carson looked at the compass on his watch, pointing NE. He was headed to Johor, and once across the bridge, Sonya would pick him up. His next call would come tonight to update his progress.

He pulled out his canteen to drink some water, and a shot rang out from a distance, piercing the metal container which shot from his hand.

"Shit!" He began running through the thick woods. He could hear the dirt bikes coming in his direction. He could see a large structure above the trees and started running towards it. He pulled his 1911 from his side and hid behind a northern red oak as they neared. He fired several shots and destroyed the bike's front wheel, sending the rider into a tree.

The other stopped his bike and pulled an M4A1 from his back, shooting a hole into a branch. The wounded limb fell, missing Carson's head.

He thought that golfing at The Pines would be so much better than this shit. The Observation tower was now less than a few hundred yards away, and he needed a diversion.

Carson dug through his bag, found a flash grenade, and began to zig and zag through the trees. The rider started his bike and began to chase Carson. As the motorcycle gained on his position, Carson threw the flash grenade, and the stunned the rider ditched his bike.

Carson made his way up the stairs of the observation deck, trying to get to the highest position. He crouched between the railings for a moment and searched for his attacker. He could see the masked man run up behind a tree close to the tower. His attacker radioed to someone, and then he pulled his rifle and fired a bullet that pierced Carson's pack.

"I don't suppose you have a smoke on you?" Carson yelled at the assailant.

The answer was two bullets that pinged off the railings.

"I'm going to take that as a no!" he yelled back. This was not Mr. G's gangster. No, this was a trained killer. Carson needed to think about his next step to get out of this area alive.

He rolled over and dug in his bag, finding some binoculars. Another shot rang out, and concrete exploded near his feet. He moved again to a safe position on his stomach. He could see the shooter's rifle sticking out from the tree, and beside the tree was his dirt bike. He pulled his 1911 and began firing at the motorcycle, destroying the tire. The gunman fired a bullet, which whistled at him. Carson fired three more shots, and the bike blew up and sent the man flying.

"Bullseye." Carson waived his fist and could see the attacker's posse heading his way in the distance. He ran down the stairs of the tower, and just as he got to the bottom, he ducked behind a concrete slab. A truck just pulled near the front. It was a local ranger of the park, and he was on his truck radio.

"We have a fire in the park, and we need engines here now!" he yelled. The ranger grabbed a fire extinguisher and began to run towards the burning bike to put it out.

"No, get down, Ranger Rick" he yelled. The man turned and saw Carson for the first time. Then he turned back to put out the fire, pulled the pin to the extinguisher, and started spraying the fire. Smoke began to rise, and the ranger backed up. However, he did not notice the masked attacker lying in the grass to his left.

"For Christ's sake, man, get down!" Carson yelled again.

The gunman leaned up, pulled a Glock from his side, and pointed it at the ranger. He was about to pull the trigger when the bullet passed through his chest.

The startled ranger stopped spraying the fire and fell to the ground. He looked back to see Carson standing in a crouched position with his gun pointed in his direction.

"Please don't kill me!" the ranger screamed.

"I won't, but he almost killed you!" Carson yelled back. "You need to go and hide and wait for the fire engines to arrive. I am going to borrow your truck, okay?"

"Yes, yes, sir," the frightened ranger yelled back.

Carson jumped into the Chevrolet and fired it up. He began to drive out of the park. If assumptions were correct, he would have less than 30 minutes to find a safe zone before Mr. G's goons or the SPF located him. As he turned onto Tank Road, he could see flashing lights in his rearview mirror.

CHAPTER 40

"Will this be a quick procedure, nurse?" Jacob asked.

"About 45 minutes now that we are all prepped. The nurse explained that your wife was given an epidural and will not feel anything from the midsection down to her feet," the nurse explained.

"Will we be able to hold the baby after it's born?" he asked.

"Of course, after the baby responds, usually with a cry. And then once we clean and swaddle the baby," she said.

Janet pulled down the oxygen mask and looked in Jacob's direction.

"Babe, enough with the questions. I want to have our baby," she cajoled.

The anesthesiologist walked in, grabbed a chart, and looked at a monitor. Then he looked at his watch.

"Mrs. Jordon, how do you feel or not feel?" he jested.

"I feel tired and ready to have this baby," she said.

"Dr. Gillette, I believe we are ready to get started," he said.

A curtain was placed just above her sternum, and Jacob nor Janet could see the procedure taking place. Jacob was told earlier by the nurse that there would be two incisions made at her navel, and then a three-inch incision would be made in the wall of her uterus, and the baby would be removed.

"Nurse, I need a BP update," Dr. Gillete said.

"Still looking good, doctor, at 140/90," she answered.

"Making incision one, team," Dr. Gillete said.

The heart monitor and other electronics beeps made Jacob uneasy during the procedure, and he saw that Janet had some uncomfortable moments.

He made the second incision moments later, and then pulled out their son. The nurses took the baby to a station that had an overhead heating light and spanked its bottom. He began crying.

"Mom and Dad, we have a healthy baby. Do you have a name in mind?" one of the attending nurses asked.

Janet pulled down the oxygen mask and looked at Jacob as they said it in unison.

"Jeremy Maxwell Jordon."

The nurses cleaned and swaddled Jeremy and brought him to see Janet, who wiped tears from her eyes. They placed him on her chest to hold. Jacob was smiling widely.

"Jacob Jordon, are you crying?" Janet laughed.

"Tears of joy, my love. Tears of joy."

The nurses picked up the baby, and the doctor began to repair the incisions.

"I don't feel well," Janet said to Jacob. And he heard the beep of her heart change.

"Dr. Gillette, her blood pressure is crashing," the attending said.

"Take Mr. Jordon out of the surgical area," the doctor instructed.

"What is going on? Is Janet okay?" he said and saw his wife's face turn pale. "Janet... Janet—I love you."

As they nearly pushed him out of the surgery, he could hear one loud, clear tone and people scrambling.

Moments later, he was in the waiting room with Janet's parents.

"Edwin and Teresa, we had a boy named Jeremy Maxwell Jordon," his voice trembled, and tears fell from his eyes. "Janet went into cardiac arrest, and they pushed me out of the room. They will provide an update shortly."

"Dear God," Teresa said and began to faint. Edwin and Jacob helped her to a seat. They all hugged for a moment, and then Jacob asked if they could pray. They grabbed hands.

"God, we thank you that you never leave us, that you never forsake us, but you love us. We trust you and pray this in your name. Amen," Edwin said, and then there was silence between them.

CHAPTER 41

The large green sign read:
Singapore Zoo 1 KM
Johor Bahar Bridge 12 KM
Carson needed to pull over and hide the truck in the brush. At this moment, he expected the SPF, Chinese MSS agents, and Mr. G's gang to be hunting him down. He pulled over, finding a tree and a large bush. He grabbed his bag and pulled out the satellite phone, which had a hole in it. It would not light up.

"Damn it!" Carson screamed. He looked at his watch and turned the dial counterclockwise. The dial lit up red and beeped, turning green. This sent a location update to Sonya. He pondered how his attackers found him in a very remote area of the park. Could his go-bag be infected with a tracker?

Carson emptied the bag and inventoried his weapons. He searched each area and did not detect a device sewn into the bag. He had a green surplus bag inside and decided to ditch the go-bag and loaded the ammo, grenades, first aid kit, and rations.

He walked until he entered the grounds of the zoo. He hid behind a tree, pulled out his electronic binoculars, scoped the terrain, and determined his best point of entry was a side gate of the property. He put away the binoculars and dug out a change of clothes. He put on a black T-shirt and black tactical ridge pants with his gun and knife belt, and he wore a jacket as the temperature would begin to drop overnight.

His pace was fast and deliberate to a huge green fence. He pulled out a fence cutter, snipped six pieces, and entered the property. Carson wondered in which area he was entering and hoped it was not a pen with a dangerous animal.

* * *

"You imbecile! Stop talking and go find him!" the commander said. "I will update his coordinates by pager."

His next call was to the SPF captain.

"Captain Wang," the commander said firmly.

"Commander, the wire was confirmed for $550,000. Your donation is appreciated. We are in pursuit of the target and will bring this criminal to justice," Wang said.

"Good doing business with you, Captain," the commander said. "Once you have him, I want to interview him, please."

"As you wish," he agreed.

* * *

Carson remembered visiting the zoo with an associate. This particular zoo has an open concept with its animals. The environment is much like a rainforest and has over 300 species. What needed to be considered was to not trek upon an animal's habitat.

As he walked and looked at the Orangutans, several police officers ran up and down the streets. They were looking for Carson, whose disguise must have worked. Before ditching it, he wore a hat, sunglasses with a long wig, and a fake mustache from his go-bag. He also grabbed a special sandwich made for him by the church. He had added an extra layer to the sandwich. He took a bite from the corner and put it in his pocket for a moment.

Darkness was settling on the zoo, and soon they would close their gates. He determined that finding the penguins may be a good place to lay low and began making his way to the aquarium. Mr. G's gang members bumped into Carson near the crocodile expedition.

"That's him," one said, and five of the members made a circle around him.

"Are you sure you want to accept my dance card?" Carson said sarcastically.

The men rushed him, and he kneed the first in the groin, pushed him into another, and took out another with a roundhouse kick. One jumped him and held his arms behind his back as the others began to punch him.

"Hey, why don't you pick on someone your size," a small woman said to the gang members who wore a symbol on their wrists.

"Don't make me laugh, bitch," he said.

"I am not here to tickle your funny bone...just to send you home crying," she said.

Carson recognized her voice.

"Tang?" he asked.

One of the men came running at her with a knife and tried to stab her. She grabbed his wrist and flipped him to the ground, kicking him in the jaw and knocking him out cold.

The others kept punching Carson and tried to take his bag, but Tang pulled her Glock with a silencer. She took a shot and missed. The image was effective. Everyone ran from the area.

"Thanks, Tang," Carson said. "But I thought you were traveling."

"I was, but I got called out on assignment," she replied.

"Are you here to help?" he said.

"Yeah, I think I already did that, man," she said.

As they began to walk, Carson noticed a police helicopter with a spotlight searching the zoo. The light shined down on both of them.

"Stay where you are, or we will fire," the SPF said across a loudspeaker.

The SPF was surrounding the area as the call went out from the helicopter.

"I used to work here as a teenager before I got into this crazy line of work as an agent," she said. "We need to take a passage past the aquarium to an exit side gate leading to the parking lot. When I say run, you are going to follow me through this group of trees. Got it?"

"Got it," Carson said.

"Run!" she said. Carson headed into the rainforest but threw his sandwich to the crocodiles to munch upon. Shots rained from above, killing a bird and mangling a tree.

"I was headed to the aquarium, but I am sure I would have gotten lost," he said, impressed.

"Just keep running, Carson, we have a way to go, and they will be following us."

They ran for nearly 10 minutes and covered half of the habitats. Tang slowed, and she pointed to the aquarium to the west side of the property as they were headed northeast.

"Yes, you would have been lost," she said. "How the hell did you get yourself in this mess of blowing up your house and killing that kid?"

"What do you mean 'kid?'" he asked.

"Well, they did the autopsy, and they determined he was 16 years old. He had a record working for Mr. G."

"They did an autopsy already?" he asked.

"Yes, this is serious, and SPF has a reward for your capture," she said.

"I didn't know he was a kid," he said. "There were three of them, and one was as big as a linebacker. I couldn't have known he was so young."

"What did they want?" she asked.

"Highly classified documents which need to be returned to Langley HQ," he said.

"Did you break cover, Carson?" she asked.

"No. I entered information into my computer on NSFNET, and it triggered an alert all over the screen. I knew I got caught in the black net."

"So, what did you do with the information?" she asked.

"Trying to get it to Sonya," he said. "I am glad you showed."

"Were you trying to escape Singapore?" she asked.

"Yes, with some help into Indonesia," he said. "Thankfully, Sonya reached you to get me to the rendezvous point, right?"

The sun had set, and darkness was upon them. They had walked through several habitats. As they exited the gate to the parking lot, a bright light blinded Carson.

"No. Sonya never called me, Carson. I'm sorry," she said.

"Huh, what do you mean you're sorry?" he said, and Tang turned quickly and hit him with the butt of her gun in the head.

"Sleep well," she said.

Tang pulled out her cell and dialed a number.

"Commander, I have him, and I will bring him in under one condition," Tang said.

"Good, and what's that, agent?" the commander asked.

"The cash you promised, and don't kill him," she said.

"I have your reward waiting at the old penal settlement," he said. "Get to the harbor with the coordinates I'm paging you and take the boat. I need him alive."

"Never thought being a double agent would pay this good. I hope this is worth it, commander," she replied.

"It is. It is..." And he hung up.

CHAPTER 42

Wilkerson's clothes were drenched, and he believed he had a concussion from hitting the steering wheel on impact. He waited at the riverbank for a few hours contemplating his next move. The shooters were Asian, and they were after Elizabeth, but they took off in their damaged Mercedes after the crash.

About that time, he made his way to find a pay phone, which happened to be by a liquor store. Wilkerson punched in the digits to CIA headquarters and asked to speak with Director Cookson.

"Wilkerson?" Cookson asked.

"Yes, sir. We are not on a secure line," Wilkerson said.

"Any news on the expat delivery?" Cookson asked.

"Secured and then compromised," Wilkerson admitted. "Burned by dissidents on country soil," he said.

"Find a safe zone and report back in at that time," he said.

Wilkerson hung up the phone and flagged down a taxi.

"26 Federal Plaza, please," he said to the driver.

"Name is Casselli, boss, and you can be sure I will get you there right away," he said. "How about them Rangers last night?"

"I am not a sports fan," Wilkerson said.

"Yeah, yeah, I get you. You a movie fan because you just saw a phenomenal flick?" Casselli asked.

"Not really. No, but I do like firing my guns at targets."

The driver's eyes widened, and then he grunted. The rest of the ride was silent.

* * *

Tang had two of Mr. G's members help place Carson in the boat after searching him.

"No disk," Pang said.

"Nah. We didn't find anything," one of the members said.

"Where is his bag?" she asked.

"What bag, Tang?" he questioned.

"The black bag he was carrying," she said.

"He didn't have it when we reached you," he answered.

"Go back and search through the zoo and find it," she requested.

The trip to the abandoned Crescent prison was a short ride. The prison had a lookout tower and was known for wild gusts of wind from the straits of Johor. It was enclosed by high concrete walls covered with barbed wire at the top to stop prisoners from escaping.

"There was no electronic device on Carson," she said to Mr. G, standing above Carson.

"That is too bad, really," he said and formed his fist into a ball and punched Carson. Carson was tied to the chair, and the punch's force sent the chair to the ground.

"Thank you," Carson said as two muscular men picked up the chair to set him upright. He spit blood on their shoes. His face was bruised, and fingers were bloody as they had pulled off his nails.

"What is going on?" Tang said. "I was told you were not going to hurt him or kill him."

"Depends if he decides to hand over the device or not," Mr. G said.

"What device?" Carson mumbled with a very swollen mouth and right eye.

"Jesus, Carson, what are you thinking?" Tang asked.

Carson looked at her with a wild, angry stare.

"Traitor," he said. "You won't break me. You can make me bleed, but you can't take my virtue, pride, or patriotic spirit. I took an oath."

"Turn on the camera and video record this," Mr. G said. "He's our good old western hero."

* * *

"That promotion should have been mine already," Wilkerson said. "I called to tell you I need the data. No more games."

Wilkerson looked around the room to ensure no other agents listened to his conversation. After his wife was killed, he became reclusive, narcissistic, anxious, and nearly quit the CIA.

"I don't care how you get it. Just get it done," he said. "We are on a deadline."

He nearly slammed the phone in the cubicle he had borrowed from Agent Jefferson D. Davis. He thought of Jordon and wanted to find her. He watched as she swam to the opposite side and collapsed.

The Jacob J. Javits building housed some of the best CIA analysts on the planet to help research and run interference. In the public's eye, this building staffs the General Services Administration.

He walked to Hal Hallahan's office and sat down. Hal was the lead analyst and could access almost any detail on any citizen or foreign national in America.

"Director Cookson said you would be stopping by," Hal said.

"I am sure he did. I need you to research where Elizabeth Jordon is at this very moment. Hotels, trailer parks, family residences, churches, etc.," he said.

"Sir, before I start tracking Mrs. Jordon, I think you should see this," Hal said.

"See what, Hallahan?" Wilkerson replied.

Hallahan stood up and picked up a large envelope off his desk, dug inside it, and pulled a VHS tape inserted into a video cassette player.

"This arrived overnight at Langley and our location," he said. He turned on the television and hit play on the machine.

"Jesus! This is worse than I thought. They have Agent Jordon, and he looks in bad shape. Have we tracked where this originated?" Wilkerson asked.

"Singapore, sir," Hal responded.

"Find the expat, Hallahan," Wilkerson said.

Hal sat down at his desk, punched a few keys, and looked up at Wilkerson.

"How about her Aunt Estelle's house?" he asked.

"Get me an address and give me that tape," he said. "We got a trip to take."

"Sir?" Hallahan said.

"Call me Chief Wilkerson, agent," he replied.

"Chief, I haven't been trained to be a field agent. Are you sure there isn't someone else you could bring?"

Hallahan was a native of New York and had just completed training at the farm with the CIA as a blue folder agent. He was considered a top-notch analyst. He found Elizabeth Jordon in less than two minutes, and that impressed Wilkerson.

"Kid, you're as good as it gets. Keep your mouth shut until I need you," he told Hallahan.

CHAPTER 43

Elizabeth leaned against the back of the shower as the hot water warmed her body. She pondered how her injuries hurt less than before. She believed the extreme cold temperatures of the river had something to do with this experience. This thought was blocking the urge to process why these events were happening.

Elizabeth faced the shower and began to sob. She wanted to scream for the souls lost, saving her life in the past 24 hours. She scrubbed at her skin as if to wash away the guilt. She couldn't purge the images of death.

"You will not be forgotten, William Garse, Agent Matthews, Agent Danielson, and Chief Danielson," she mumbled and then prayed.

May your holy water cleanse me of my sins, dear Father. May Christ, who was crucified for you, bring you freedom and peace.

May Christ who died for you admit you into his garden of paradise. May Christ, the true Shepherd, embrace you as one of his flock.

She was so thankful for her Aunt Estelle. She was the youngest of her mother's family. She was so supportive after Elizabeth's parents had passed. Elizabeth sat on the edge of the bed and picked up a pair of denim jeans, black T-shirt, and boots Estelle had laid out. It was nearly 1 p.m. and she had slept almost six hours. But sleeping during this time of day upset her body's time clock.

Elizabeth dressed, brushed her teeth, and battled, combing her wet and tangled long hair.

"Cherie?" said Cynthia as she knocked on the door.

"Yes, come in," she replied.

"Are you hungry?" Cynthia asked.

"Starved and so tired," she replied.

"Chicken noodle soup is good for the soul, Cherie," Cynthia said with a smile.

"Then soup du jour it is!" Elizabeth said. "Cynthia, has Carson called recently?"

"I am not sure... I was gone the past few days. And I am not sure if Estelle has checked her machine. She was panicked when you didn't call. I imagine she had to check it," Cynthia said.

"Where is my aunt?" she asked.

"After she got you settled, she went and laid down. I believe she might be sleeping. She had not slept in 24 hours."

"Poor thing," Elizabeth said. "Thankfully, I was able to reach her after my night. I think I was drunk. I caught a bus and got off too early. I was near the edge of a river and fell in. I walked for miles to find a phone to call my aunt."

"Wow! Estelle had not told me this, Cherie," Cynthia said. "I think you should lay down, and I will bring you the soup and take your vitals after this, Elizabeth."

"Seriously? I am fine," she responded but interrupted the doorbell ringing and then several knocks on the door.

"Carson!" she said and ran past Cynthia and down the stairs to answer the front door. She felt as if she nearly ripped the door off the hinges when she swung the door open.

"Hi, Elizabeth," Holt said.

Elizabeth stood staring at Holt. He had sandy brown hair, blue eyes, and broad shoulders. His physique fit well with his 6'3" height.

"Those are some large saucers coming at me. Are you okay, Elizabeth?" he said.

"Forgive me. It's just that I was trying to remember something," she said. "How are you? Wait. How did you know I was here? Why are you here?"

"I wish I were here under better conditions," he said. "It's Carson... He has been kidnapped!"

"What?" Elizabeth nearly screamed and remembered her aunt.

"Elizabeth, may I come in please?" he asked.

"Yes, come in," she said.

"Cherie, are you all right?" Cynthia asked from the kitchen. "Who is at the front door?"

"An old friend of Carson's. Give me a moment, okay?" Elizabeth said.

"Okay, would your friend like a refreshment?" she asked.

"Um, no, thank you," he said.

"Come in the living room, Colonel," Elizabeth said.

"Elizabeth, I am no longer part of the military. I was undercover for a while. Cliff Holt was my code name. While we are not supposed to reveal our identities, I feel this is different. My name is Zachary Minh. Just call me Zack."

"Zack, huh? Okay. How do you know Carson has been kidnapped and why?" she asked.

"Because I received a call from Carson, and then a videotape was sent to me by my superiors," he said.

"Superiors?" she asked.

"Elizabeth, I know your background as an expat and your honorable service to this country. Your husband and I served together in the military, as you know, but I recruited him into the CIA. We lost touch after I was sent on a mission."

"CIA?" she asked with a puzzled face.

"Your husband has been one of the best field officers for the agency," Holt said.

"He's a golf engineer, Cliff. Ugh, I mean Zack," she responded.

"His cover, I am afraid," he replied.

"No. Did he put you up to this?" she asked.

"This is no prank. He is in real trouble, and we need to get to Singapore to meet Sonya."

"Sonya?" she asked. "You know Sonya?"

"Yes, we have served on several missions together," he said.

"Forgive me, I have to sit down," she said. "I am really in the dark here, Zack, and confused."

"Sonya reached out to me and told me I might find you here," Holt explained. "The videotape is from Carson's captors, and they have beaten him."

"But why?" she asked.

"Harbinger," he said.

She sat silently for a moment with tears rolling down her cheeks. Kal had died to protect the information on the disk. Now Carson must have found it while packing the house.

"You know about Harbinger?" she asked.

"Yes, it's my job to know about Harbinger. The information on the disk is critical to the safety of all U.S. citizens."

"I know. I have spent the last 24 hours running from some Asian group trying to kill me. They killed three agents and a civilian who helped me escape."

"What? Do you have the disk?" he asked.

"No, but someone thought I did. I met him at the theater last night, and they killed him."

"Elizabeth, you need to get your things together quickly. Everyone is looking for your husband. Your condo burned down, and someone was killed in the fire. The Singapore police and government agency are searching for him. I imagine the Chinese agents are behind his kidnapping," he said.

"Okay, I will look at the next flight leaving JFK," she quipped.

"No, Elizabeth, we are going on a black ops mission," he said. "Pack a light bag of clothes and makeup. We will discuss disguises and other mission plans on the C-141 to Germany and then the next day to Singapore. Do not tell anyone where we are going. This includes your family and the housekeeper. Understand?"

"No, Cynthia, isn't my aunt's housekeeper... Oh, wait that doesn't matter. I understand. But, please, wait outside so I can gather my things and create a reason for leaving."

"Sounds good," he said and walked out the front door.

Elizabeth turned to look at the answering machine, which had a blinking red light. She ran over and pressed the button.

"Mom, it's Jacob. Congratulations, you and dad are now grandparents of Jeremy Maxwell Jordon. I don't have much time to speak because Janet is in intensive care after her blood pressure plummeted when Jeremy was born. We are at Christ Hospital, so call me."

BEEP. She pushed the button again, and Carson had left a message. Tears streamed down Elizabeth's face. She deleted the message.

"I'm on my way, honey," she said.

* * *

Elizabeth walked out the front door and down the porch steps to a black convertible Porsche.

"Nice ride," Elizabeth said.

"Thanks. It's a 9-11 Porsche with an adjustable wing," Zack answered as he put his foot on the pedal. The tires squealed. The feeling of a fast car was something she enjoyed. Carson's Mustang had the same kind of muscle, and their dates came with some immediate action on the road. In the front seat, she remembered.

A sense of fear came over Elizabeth. *How are we going to find Carson? What happens if we don't get there in time?* She tried to convince herself it would be okay, but she regretted having gone to Hong Kong and being stuck at the airport only to have top secret information passed along to her. She had a high level of adrenaline and felt twitchy. She did not know Zack well other than the badge he showed up entering the house.

"Where is our next stop?" Elizabeth asked.

"I have a storage area where I keep my rations, weapons, and other items needed for Missions. Before we get there, we will stop at a local drug store, and I want you to buy some red hair dye, dark sunglasses, and a hat. I hear you have a talent with disguises."

"I have had my training with makeup and prosthetics," Elizabeth said. "I have two fake passports ready without photos a cobbler created for us. Once we arrive in Germany, we will need to find quarters to do our makeup and take photos. I will have my contact in Germany finish the process. This mission is not on the books, Elizabeth, so if anything happens to either of us, it will not be reported. Understood?"

"Got it." Elizabeth's heart was pounding. She had never served in the field. But saving her husband was her number one priority. Besides, Sonya would be meeting her.

* * *

The black Buick pulled to the curb and parked. Wilkerson got out and walked around the front of the car.

"Stay!" Wilkerson barked at Hallahan as if he were commanding a dog.

"No problem, Chief," Hallahan said, saluting him.

Wilkerson rang the doorbell and Cynthia answered the door.

"Hello, can I help you?" she said in a New Orleans draw.

"I am Chief Agent Wilkerson, and I am looking for Elizabeth, please?"

"Agent, huh? Where's your credential, big dog?" she asked with wide eyes.

He dug into his wallet, pulled out a card, and handed it to her.

"I am here on urgent business. Is she around so that we could speak?" he asked.

"She was resting after an accident but just left with another fella heading to pick up Carson at the airport."

"That is not possible," he said.

"Of course, it is possible," Cynthia said. "They left in his souped-up car."

"Who is that at the door, Cynthia?" asked Estelle, who woke up at the sound of the doorbell.

"Some man in a black suit and tie is asking for your niece," Cynthia said.

Estelle walked in and pushed Cynthia aside.

"Listen here, fellow, I already spoke with the police this morning," she said.

"I am sorry, I think you have me confused with the police. I am not local," he said. "I have worked with your niece while in Asia."

"Oh, in Singapore, huh?" Estelle said.

"No, in China while serving her country as an expat," Wilkerson said.

"Expat? My niece?" she said with the grin of a Cheshire cat.

"Yes. And this is why I am here. Carson has been kidnapped, and I have a video to show her and confirm his identity."

"You're lying, and I find this outrageous," she said.

"Is she here or not?" he asked again.

Cynthia was in the background on her cell phone with someone, and Wilkerson focused on the call.

"Yeah, there's a man flashing some CIA card. What should we do?" Cynthia asked the other person on the phone.

"Okay, listen, your niece may be in danger, and her husband, as I mentioned, had an incident in Singapore. If she is not here, I will be going," Wilkerson said, looking down at Estelle's stare.

"She's not. As I told you, some good-looking guys came here, and they left. Elizabeth must have known him. She said he was an old friend of Carson," Cynthia said as she held the phone to her ear. "Yeah, they are leaving. I think we are good."

"Cynthia, you did not tell me Elizabeth left. Does she have her phone on her? We need to find where she went if not to the airport. Something doesn't sound right. Did he say expat?" Estelle asked as she closed the door on Wilkerson.

"Old bag," he said, walked to the car, and got in. Hallahan had his head down, reading a book.

"Hallahan, wake up. Time to see how good of an analyst you are," Wilkerson said and drove off.

* * *

The Porsche roared down the freeway at high speed. For three hours, Elizabeth and Zack talked. She told him about her new grandson and her travels as an expat, and how she met Carson. But she had questions about his time in the military and now had many questions regarding his involvement with the CIA. "We met in basic training and hit it off. I got my degree and went to officer's school. We kept in touch until the CIA approached me. I did my training for a year without reaching out to anyone. Once I was free to roam again, I reached out to Carson and recruited him into the agency," Zack explained. "We lost touch again when he went away to train as an intelligence officer."

"I wonder why he didn't tell me about the CIA when we first started dating?" she said.

"Sworn to secrecy. Also, to protect you, I imagine," he said. "It didn't help I was involved in a training accident before a mission."

The Porsche sped up to the gate, and an enlisted guard saluted him, waved them through, and opened the gate. Zack revved the car and accelerated, and they drove along the runway. The sun was setting against dark clouds, and the wind was blowing. Zack pulled up to the camouflaged painted C-141. The loading crew pulled out a tread ramp, and Zack pulled the car onto the plane.

"Thanks, men, for securing her," he said. "We'll change plates at our final destination."

"Time to go?" Elizabeth asked.

"Elizabeth, grab your bag and go sit in the webbed seats. The Master Chief will get you secured," he said.

Zack walked over to the seating, dropped his pack, opened it, pulled out a satellite phone, looked at his watch, and dialed a number. Elizabeth watched but could not hear as the plane's generator to start the engines kicked in.

"Ma'am, I need you to buckle in this belt so we can secure you," he said. His name tag read *Sorenson*.

"Thank you, Master Chief Sorenson."

"My pleasure. We will taxi here at 1900 hours with a flight time of 6 hours and 30 minutes," he said.

"Thank you," she said and turned to see Zack's face turning red and yelling at someone. He pushed a button and walked over to sit next to Elizabeth.

"You okay?" she asked.

"What do you mean?" he replied.

"You seemed to have a pretty intense call," she said.

"Some details which should have been handled for our trip. But don't mix up my aggression with my passion for my friend and your husband. I want to make sure this operation doesn't go belly up. Carson is naked and has no support until we rendezvous with Sonya."

CHAPTER 44

The briefing room was buzzing in Langley. Cookson was watching the BBC reports of police surrounding the local zoo to hunt down the alleged American killer of a Singaporean.

"Which agents are on the ground in Singapore?" Cookson asked.

An analyst stood up and addressed the question. "Sir, agent Testalova has reported in since receiving a call from Jordon, who went dark nearly 24 hours ago."

Cookson pulled his cell phone out of his jacket and dialed Wilkerson.

"Hello, director," Wilkerson answered.

"Have you located Elizabeth Jordon?" he asked.

"I believe she is traveling with one of our ghost agents. And they may be heading to Singapore based on flight information leaving from Dover," he explained.

"Then I am clearing you to take a jet I will have prepared for you to fly to Singapore. We are in contact with agent Testalova and will coordinate and intercept."

"Sir, my analyst has determined the Chinese have rolled up agent Jordon," Wilkerson said. "I am working with analyst Hallahan, and his team is monitoring chatter coming from phone calls."

"If agent Jordon has the Harbinger file, this cannot get into enemy hands. Am I understood?" he said sternly.

"Yes, sir. Can you please page me coordinates for my flight out? Also, I like to take Hallahan with me. He is a great resource, sir," Wilkerson requested.

"Fine with me. He is your responsibility," the director answered.

* * *

Elizabeth had fallen asleep within 10 minutes of takeoff for several hours.

"I'm sorry I fell asleep," she said.

She pondered for a moment on her last dream. The man in the dream was not Carson but someone whom she felt passionately about. She could not remember the details of their adventure, but she did remember he was killed. This upset her so much that she nearly drowned in a bathtub after drinking two bottles of wine. She remembered being submerged under the water and falling asleep until she woke on Zack's shoulder.

"It's okay, Elizabeth. Glad my shoulder served some purpose today," Zack said.

"Crew, please prepare for the landing in Ramstein," the captain said.

Once on the ground, the ramp was lowered. A cold wind whipped snow inside, hitting Elizabeth in the face. She shivered.

"You're going to need your jacket tonight," Zack warned. "There are expected freezing temperatures and perhaps one of the coldest nights at –15 degrees."

"Thanks," she said and put on her black peacoat. It was nearly one o'clock in the morning, and they needed to sleep. The barracks had an area with two beds, but one was without a blanket. Zack offered the bed, but Elizabeth said they could share it. He pulled off his coat and his wool sweater. Zack's T-Shirt rolled up, and she could see a beautiful array of colors from what looked like a tattoo.

"That's a lot of ink," she said.

"Yeah, I got it while traveling and I've been adding to it," he said.

"Can I see it?" she asked.

"It's not done yet, and quite frankly, that's bad luck," Zack said.

They slept back-to-back in the small bunk with a pillow in between them. The thought of sleeping with another man after being with Carson for so long felt weird. Zack fell asleep quickly, and his breathing was light. She listened to his breathing and soon began to dream of Carson.

Sirens blasted outside of the barracks, and Elizabeth put out her hand, trying to push the alarm to snooze, but it wasn't there. She felt an arm around her, snuggling her breast. She waited so long to have Carson here next to her, but as the drowsiness wore off, she realized it was Zack.

"Hey, do you mind!" she said, facing him.

He leaned up close to her face and kissed her on the lips. The kiss was warm and familiar. The experience was electric and made the hair on her arms rise. And then she realized who was kissing her.

"Wow, just as I remember it," Zack said.

"Colonel Holt!" Elizabeth yelled. "I was told you died in a parachuting accident."

"I did for the CIA. And I had to die for you, Elizabeth," he said.

"I went to your damn funeral! I cried for weeks and began drinking again," Elizabeth said. She jumped off the bed and started pacing.

"Hey, remember, it's Zack Minh?" he said. "That other name was an operational name."

"I don't care what it was, Zacharia!" she said.

He stood and tried to assuage her by hugging her, and as he leaned close, she slapped him so hard her hand ached.

"I guess I deserved that," he said.

"You did. I'm married and love Carson," she exclaimed.

"I understand and apologize," he said. "Carson is still a friend, and I would never dishonor him."

Elizabeth's emotions were twisted. Her hormonal desire was for Zack, but her heart belonged to Carson. Zack's eyes were fixed on her, and then he looked at his watch.

"When do we leave for Singapore?" she asked.

"0800, Elizabeth. We have two hours to prepare. You need to dye your hair and apply the disguise we discussed on our ride to Dover.

"We'll talk later, but let's go save my husband!" she said.

* * *

"We just landed on a remote strip about 10KM from Singapore," he said. "It is an hour from the city, and we will need to talk about our next steps to get what we need."

He put away the satellite phone and spoke to the operations chief.

"The plates and passports ready?" he asked.

"Plates are on your vehicle with registration," Sorenson said and handed him the passports with pictures.

"Good job, Chief," he said. "The black and white photos are perfect!"

"Thank you, sir!" Sorenson said.

"Let's go, expat, we need to meet some important people," Zack said.

She walked to the Porsche, got into the seat, and slammed the door.

"Easy now. Save that aggression for your hubby's kidnappers," he replied.

They drove in silence until they reached the heart of the city.

"I need you to do me a favor, please," she said. "I need to go to my local church, Sacred Heart."

"We are really short on time, Elizabeth, and we need to meet my contact," he growled.

"I understand, but I think I may know how we can find Carson," she retorted.

"Okay, co-pilot, give me the coordinates," he said with a smirk.

* * *

The Porsche pulled into an empty parking lot, and Elizabeth opened the door, grabbed her pack, and turned to Zack.

"I won't be long," she said. "And no offense, but I have a letter to bring to our local priest." She closed the door and headed into the church.

Near the altar, she found a nun who was kneeling and had a lit a candle. Elizabeth genuflected, made the sign of the cross, and knelt next to the sister.

"Excuse me, sister, can you tell me how I could find Father Linly?" she whispered.

"Yes, dear, but it may be hard to speak with him during the sacrament of reconciliation."

"Yes, thank you. This is what I need to do. Confession is uplifting. Praise God," she said.

A parish member exited the confessional, and Elizabeth entered.

"Bless me, Father, for I have sinned," she said.

"And what sins would you confess, young lady?" Joe said.

"My husband is lost in Singapore, and thoughts of another mind have clouded my soul. I love Carson!"

"Elizabeth?" Joe whispered.

"Yes, Father Joe," she whispered back.

"I absolve you of your sins. You will pray with your rosary and meet me in the rectory."

* * *

Sonya's watch beeped. It was time to call back to HQ in Langley. She had a better position where Carson may be held to inform the director.

"Is Director Cookson in his office, Ms. Sawyer?" Sonya asked.

"I will get him on a secure line immediately, agent Testarov. Please hold," she replied.

"Sonya?" Cookson said with a yawn.

"We have the coordinates, sir, and I will send the transmission for satellite tracking. I am waiting on my team to assemble before we launch the operation," she explained.

"Station Chief Wilkerson will be arriving soon. I have instructed him to call you once he is on the soil. He will join your team. He also has one of our best analysts with him, which may be a valuable resource," the director said.

"Wilkerson. Sir, really?" she asked with intrigue.

"Yes. I know your history, Sonya, but use his tactical skills," the director instructed. "One other item. Have you come in contact with the expat Jordon?"

"Sir?" she asked.

"One of our ghost agents is running a separate mission, apparently. Have you ever worked with agent Holt?"

"I have heard of him. He was part of Operation Tiger Claw and the Harbinger file," she said.

"Yes, there were four of them. He went underground after riots occurred in the streets of Hong Kong. The CCP had his photo, so we have moved him to a ghost role."

"So, what is he doing here with the musician?" she asked.

"He has a background working with intelligence officer Jordon. They were excellent friends until Holt went underground. I imagine he is trying to find Jordon and make a deal with the terrorists. He is a ghost, and there isn't much more I can tell you."

"We have to play with the cards we are dealt," she retorted. "I guess he will have to find Jordon first. I have his location at the old Crescent prison. Once assembled, we will observe and report back."

CHAPTER 45

Wilkerson's plane landed at Paya Lebar Airbase in Singapore. As he walked down the stairs of the private jet, the pager to his side began to vibrate.

The Co. transport is waiting. Crescent holding tank. Prepare for an angry Leopard.

Wilkerson saw the car approaching and waved his hand at Hallahan to hurry down the stairs.

"Hallahan, I just want to remind you that we are operating on foreign soil. If the operation is a bag and burn and authorities capture you, you are a civilian in the wrong place at the wrong time. Understand?" he asked.

"Loud and clear," Hallahan said.

On the boat, Wilkerson grabbed his bag and put on his field gear. He holstered his 1911 with a Marine insignia handle and prepared Hallahan on Sonya's background and the mission.

"Excuse me, sir," Hallahan said as he ran to the side of the boat and became sick.

* * *

"Joe, I am in trouble, and I need your help," Elizabeth said. "Carson has been kidnapped, and he may have a file that could save his life. I am willing to make a trade with his kidnappers."

"Carson was here several days ago and handed me an envelope I was just about to mail. I assume this is what you're looking for?" Joe handed it to her.

Elizabeth ripped open the package and there was a book inside. She opened the cover and flipped the pages until a secret compartment revealed half of the disk.

"Why are people searching for a broken disk?" she pondered. "No matter, I need to ensure this is returned safely."

She noticed she had the top half of the disk, and there was a slider at the top, which she pushed back to see a small opening.

"Do you have black waxed shoestring?" Elizabeth asked.

"Why, yes, I have one on an old shoe you can have," Joe said and went to his private quarters and brought it back.

Elizabeth put the string through the hole, tied one end in a knot, and put it around her neck.

"Father, can I borrow your phone?"

Elizabeth dialed Sonya's international pager and sent her the number of Sacred Heart.

The phone rang instantly.

"This is the musician," Elizabeth said.

"I am sending a transport," Sonya said.

"Not here. Newton Circus Circle is better. I am a redhead now," Elizabeth said and hung up the phone.

"Father do you have a way to transport me there?" she asked.

"We have a truck transporting food to our other church, and they can drop you off along the way," he said.

"One more favor, Father, please?" she asked. "There is a black Porsche sitting in the parking lot. Once I have departed, can you please bring the driver a note? I will write him and bring a cup of coffee."

"You have a driver in a Porsche of all cars, huh?" he joked. "Yes, I will do this for your family."

* * *

Sonya, Wilkerson, and Hallahan parked the green Jeep near the entrance of the abandoned prison and split up. Sonya went to an apartment building near the prison. Wilkerson put his hoodie up and walked the street around the prison. Hallahan sat in the jeep and drew a free-hand schematic of vantage points near the prison.

"I count two shooters in the tower. One on the east and the other on the west side," Sonya said into her walkie. "When I look into the prison yard, I see approximately seven other men with AK-47s."

"I walked the prison and see one area that is not secured and maybe our way in to grab officer Jordon," Wilkerson radioed back. "Hallahan, drive the Jeep over to me, and then you can sketch this out."

"Will do," Hallahan responded.

"We will need a satellite image inside this prison and body heat images. I will call Langley to update and make that happen," Sonya said.

Several hours passed, and they all drove back to a CIA safe house. Elizabeth was waiting as they walked through the door.

"Sonya, I'm glad you're here," Elizabeth said and then noticed Wilkerson.

"You're alive!" she exclaimed. "I thought for sure after the van hit the water you...Well, I am glad you made it out."

"Good to see you too, Elizabeth," Wilkerson said.

"Okay, team, let's get to work. We need to figure out how we will get Jordon out safely."

They reviewed the satellite images sent to them and discussed creating a bigger hole in the south end of the fencing with the Jeep. But they would need a distraction at the front of the building.

"I have three team members who will be joining us shortly. One is a sniper, which we will need to take out the tower," she said.

"But what about getting into the front gate to take out the other guards?" Hallahan asked.

"I think I know how we can do that, Sonya," Elizabeth said. "What do most men like? Women, food, and beer. If we can steal a food truck and hire some local prostitutes, we may have a plan in place."

"No, I am not sure about that, Elizabeth. We could put these women in danger."

"Perhaps. But what if they serve the food to them and huddle them together? We could surround them, gather their weapons, and zip tie their hands."

"I guess it could work if none of them alerts the team inside holding Carson," Wilkerson said. "Okay, we will launch the operation at sunset. Wilkerson will take Elizabeth through the side wall opening."

A knock came at the door suddenly, and Wilkerson drew his 1911 from his side and pointed it at the door. Sonya walked over and looked out the peephole. She saw her other team members.

"Put it away, Wilkerson, it's my team," she said. Case officer Mike Rodriguez was her sharpshooter, and intelligence office Rhonda Deming was stationed in the Pacific with Tang to cover Singapore. The others were Marines flown in by Cookson.

* * *

Zack was dismayed as he drove throughout the city looking for Elizabeth. He was impressed that she pulled it off, ditching him so quickly. He had to admit the church coffee was spectacular. He pulled over and grabbed his satellite phone and made a call.

"I don't know where the expat is at this moment. We stopped, and she is now out of my custody," he said. "Stop yelling! I put a tracker in her bag, which keeps moving, and am headed in that direction. Were you able to gain the information we needed? No? We need that intelligence if we are going to win this deal."

* * *

At sundown, Sonya had briefed her team one kilometer from Crescent. The food truck, Jeep, and Hummer were on the move to the abandoned prison. They were likely to combat the Snow Leopard commandos.

"Team, we believe this group is working for the CCP. They are an elite force with special forces training and hand-to-hand combat. Shoot to eliminate the threat," Sonya commanded. "They have a distinguished mark tattooed on their body." Sonya showed them a picture.

She picked up her satellite phone and dialed HQ.

"Sir, I have reviewed the satellite images, and we believe officer Jordon is being held. Unit G cell block. The overlay of heat images identifies five bandits and one friendly seating," she said. "Permission to commence Operation Grab and Go?"

"Charlie Mike," Cookson relayed.

"Tango Mike," Sonya replied.

The green Jeep drove by Hallahan parked near the curb on the south side of the prison.

Sonya's team was in position. She served with case officer Rodriguez on multiple missions. He was perhaps the most accurate shooter she knew. He would eliminate the tower bandits and the spotlight. She also recruited and paid several women to cook and serve food to the men inside the prison. The distraction would allow the accident to occur on the south prison wall and create a bigger gap for Wilkerson's team of four members to infiltrate the prison.

Sonya was about to launch the blitz when a black Porsche turned the corner and pulled in front of the gate. The driver flashed their lights and revved the engine. The gates opened and the sports car headed into the prison.

"Hang fire, team," Sonya ordered.

"Rodriguez, I need a report on the black bogey entering Crescent," she radioed.

"Copy. Sonya, we're breaching light here. The bandit parked and was greeted by two other black hoods, over."

Rodriguez noticed through his scope that they were headed inside the prison.

"Team commences blitz," she said.

Rodriguez aimed his A40A5 at the West bandit and disabled him. The other man saw his partner fall and tried to duck, but the bullet fractured his head.

"Tower occupants are down," he said. "Go serve them up."

The food truck pulled up the gate and honked its horn. A commando pointed an AK-47 at Sonya, who was in jeans and a black T-shirt. Along with her was an attractive woman with a breast-revealing tank top.

"Please put down the gun, soldier. We brought food, drinks, and some fun. Your commander thought it would be a great surprise," Sonya suggested.

The man was a lookout, and based on his dress, Sonya surmised it was not one of the commandos. Perhaps this was the gang they hired to protect their hostage. She was now just a few feet from him, and she looked behind him to see seven men watching.

"Come out and grab food we brought from Newton Circus," one of the other women announced.

The gate opened and the men held their guns at the women. Sonya grabbed a paper dish with beef on a skewer and rice balls from one of the soldiers. He put down his weapon and grabbed the food and began to eat. The women began to serve the other seven. The eyes of the men were fixed on the scantily clad females when Sonya and two other men pointed their firearms at the men.

"Give your weapons to the women, and don't move. Kneel and put your hands behind your backs," Sonya ordered.

Her team then zip-tied each soldier's hands behind their back and walked them into the back of the food truck.

"Rodriguez, kill the light and cameras," she ordered.

Rodriguez began to take out the lights and observation cameras in the front of the building. Sonya thanked the women and dismissed them. An old grey Mercedes pulled up, and the women got in the car and drove off. Sonya revved the engine of the food truck and rammed the gate, pushing through. Soldiers from inside the prison ran out and fired upon the vehicle.

"Wilkerson, go!" Sonya radioed.

The green jeep took off down the street and ran into the weak portion of the concrete wall. The Jeep's front rollbar was destroyed and hung to the ground but had left a large enough hole for Wilkerson, Elizabeth, and two other members to run through. Hallahan backed away to the street, and Wilkerson headed through the gaping hole.

"Keep your moonbeams red, and let's move quickly," he said.

They ran through the fence and were met by hostile fire. Two soldiers heard the crash and went to inspect it.

"Rodriguez needs some help here," Elizabeth instructed.

Rodriguez could see a soldier on the grass firing at Wilkerson's team. He aimed his sight at the flash and fired. The other soldier saw the shot from Rodriguez and started firing at Rodriguez on the apartment rooftop. A bullet skimmed the drywall behind him. Elizabeth ran to where he saw the gun flash, took a knee, and fired her Glock at the soldier. He dropped to the ground.

"Push forward," Wilkerson said, waving to his team.

Elizabeth was shaking and scared. The adrenaline pushed her forward, and she ran to Wilkerson's side.

"Nice shot, Jordon," he said.

"Sonya was my trainer," she replied.

"I have never operated with a musician who puts up a good fight," he said. "Now, run!"

They entered the prison and turned off their red-light headbands. Wilkerson had a small, detailed map drawn by Hallahan. By his determination, they were in Cell Block D.

"White Russian, we are in Cell Block D approaching Cell Block G. Do you copy?"

"Roger Wilco," Sonya radioed back. "Stop moving like rainwater."

"Roger Mike," Elizabeth radioed back. Wilkerson sent Sgt. Ginny Graggario and Corporal Jason Keto ahead.

* * *

Carson wanted to sleep, and his left eye was swollen shut. The commandos had tried to obtain the information on the location of Harbinger, but he refused.

"Stop wasting your time beating him to death," Zack said as he stepped inside the cell.

"Geez, Zack. Giving up the stars and stripes for the red brigade?" Carson asked.

"Don't you start with the patriotic crap!" he yelled. "Done and done. I am looking out for myself. I'm a ghost, a hired killer for both sides. I get paid. But this is my money windfall, old friend."

"You gave up on our friendship a long time ago," Carson responded. "You're just evil now. And friends don't let other friends beat the shit out of you."

"I'm not the muscle, but I can make this worse. I want the Harbinger disk. It has the information I need to sell to the highest bidder."

"Wouldn't matter, Zack. There's two pieces to the disk, and Langley has the other piece," Carson said.

"So, I should just pull out my gun and put a bullet in your head?" Zack said as he pressed the barrel of the gun to Carson's forehead.

Zack pulled the trigger, and the gun fired and echoed through the prison. Several of the commandos ran into the cell.

"Xueboa, we are being attacked," he said.

"Hold them off and let's get Jordon out of here," the commander said. Carson was trying to regain his hearing in his left ear but heard enough of the conversation.

"Did they call you a Snow Leopard?" Carson ridiculed. "You a Chinese Leopard commando?"

"Yes, Carson, and my kill count is amazing. When you see him, you can ask Bridgewater," he said and ripped off his shirt. "Do you know what the leopard spots are called? Wait, let me tell you. Rosettes. Instead of black, I have them tattooed in red ink for each kill."

He turned to speak to another commando and ordered them to sweep the building. Carson looked at the leopard with a bird in its large mouth with fangs. Blood was dripping from its mouth. There were 15 spots colored in red. Zack turned back to Carson.

"You have a choice, Carson. You either leave with me, and we obtain the full disk in the next few days, or die right here. I don't toy with my hunt," he said. "So many others met their fate quickly."

"So, what are you waiting for exactly, Xueboa?" Carson asked.

"Don't say that name, American pig," Zack said. "You serve the country whose military killed my mother, and then I lost the person I truly loved to my best friend. That's right... Elizabeth. I brought her here, Carson, on my C-141. I kissed her, and it felt good. She will watch her husband die today."

Carson's pushed his feet to the ground and launched the chair at him.

"You son of a bitch!" he screamed. "Your mom was a bitch in heat when she had you. The U.S. soldier left her because he found out she cheated. Isn't that the true story, Zack, you never wanted to tell me? Yeah, I found out while doing my intelligence on your disappearance. That is what the CIA hired me to do."

Zack turned red and pressed the gun to Carson's leg and fired. Carson screamed in pain.

* * *

"We have penetrated the prison, and we have your six, Wilkerson," Sonya said.

"Roger, White Russian," he radioed back. "We are taking fire in Cell Block G."

Sonya and Deming were pinned down by a bandit who was firing from a higher position on the second floor.

"We need to create a diversion. I believe I can hit the fire hydrant, which is to his left. But I need to move from this prone position to my knees. Cover me when I do," Sonya instructed.

Sonya launched herself to her knees, and the shot missed the fire hydrant, and another shot rang out, killing the shooter.

"Nice job, Deming!" Sonya screamed.

"Sonya, I didn't fire my gun," she replied.

"Nope. But I did," Rodriguez said.

"You're out of position, case officer," Sonya ordered. "Glad to have you here, though. Let's go get Jordon."

They converged upon Cell Block G along with Wilkerson and his team. As they made their way to the cell where Jordon was held, a group of SPF officers surrounded them.

"Right on time, chief," Zack said, walking out of the cell. "Let's move this party to the dining hall."

"Zack!" Elizabeth screamed. "You're involved in this mess!"

"I'm the leader in creating chaos," he said.

"What did you do to my husband?"

He walked into the cell and uncuffed Carson.

"Help him to the dining hall," he ordered. The SFP pointed guns and pushed Sonya, Wilkerson, and the rest of the team down the corridor.

"I shot him and wanted to kill him because he would not give me the Harbinger file. But now I have you back, and he will give me the location of the disk."

"You mean half the disk?" she said.

"No, the whole disk," he answered. "You see, I knew you were up to something going to the church. I watched you open the book and grab the disk. I believe it's around your neck right now. Hand it over."

"Never," she replied.

Zack walked up to Elizabeth, grabbed her hair, and forced a kiss.

"Get your damn hands and mouth off of me," she said and tried to kick him. Zack whipped her leg, and she fell to the ground.

"Don't, expat. You are at a disadvantage, and I am a highly trained fighter."

In Zack's hand was the fractured disk that he removed from Elizabeth's neck during his kiss.

She jumped up and was furious with her ex-boyfriend.

"You see, the Chinese Leopard gets what he wants. Once I have the disk, I will have two pieces of information I need to finish a toxin so deadly it will wipe out the East Coast of America," he smiled.

In the dining area, they assembled the group. Sonya leaned left and whispered to Elizabeth. "Jordon, I have a flash grenade behind my back. When I give the signal, pull it, and throw it at the bandits," she said. "And one more thing. Do you remember my chapstick?"

"Yes, why?" Elizabeth whispered back.

"Grab it from my hand, and keep it as my way of saying thank you," she said.

"Thank you?" Elizabeth asked and grabbed the chapstick.

Sonya walked in front of Elizabeth and screamed at Zack.

"The infamous Chinese Leopard! You turned your back on your country after the Chinese captured you to become a double agent. Hopefully, your team understands you will turn on them," she said.

The commandos looked at each other and then at Zack.

"Fools, don't listen to this Russian hag," he said.

"So easy to fool everyone, including the Jordons. You are a traitor to everyone. He doesn't want to split the money he will get once he has his hands on the file. Let's see how much of a leader you are as the Chinese Leopard, or is it just Minh?" she asked. "Let's see you use your fighting skills against someone who can beat you."

"Sonya, the White Russian, I am half your age, and you are an excellent fighter. No, I don't want to waste any more time."

Zack lifted his Colt 9mm and shot Sonya in the chest.

"Now, Elizabeth," she said as her body crumbled.

Elizabeth grabbed the flash grenade and threw it at the enemy. The loud explosion rocked the room. Wilkerson jumped on a commando, struck him in the jaw, grabbed his AK-47, and started shooting. Deming came to his side, saw the Colt lying on the ground, and picked it up.

When the smoke cleared, SPF officers and Commandos littered the floor. The rest put down their guns and surrendered.

"Slide your weapons over to me," said Deming.

The group complied with the order. The rest of the team grabbed the weapons and formed a circle.

"Where's Zack?" Elizabeth yelled.

The Chinese Leopard was no longer in the room.

"He's a squirter, and we need to leave now," Rodriguez said. He put Sonya in a fireman's carry, and they all backed out of the dining hall. The two marines grabbed Carson, and they walked to Cell Block C and exited the Jeep.

Hallahan pulled the Jeep up and grabbed the first aid kit. Carson was bleeding from his leg and had lost a lot of blood. He was pale white. Hallahan began applying pressure and used his belt as a tourniquet. Rodriguez laid Sonya into the seat and checked her vitals. There was no heartbeat.

"She's gone," he said and ran to the Hummer parked behind the Jeep and started it. Deming helped Wilkerson carry Sonya to the Hummer and lay her in the back of the vehicle. The team split into the vehicles and headed back to the safehouse. Elizabeth held Carson as her long red hair floated in the wind. She gave him a long passionate kiss and whispered in his ear.

"Hey, Grandpa, hang on. Your grandson Jeremy Maxwell Jordon wants to meet you."

Carson smiled and nodded back.

* * *

Zack's call to his partner was unpleasant after explaining the failed mission.

"You do understand, Zack, that the CCP will find you and kill you if we don't get our hands on the other half of the disk," his partner said. "They fronted us the money for the formula we stole during our operation. The disk is the final component and the specs for the missile."

"Don't worry, I have a backup plan. But I will need your help with some information when I land back in the U.S. I will call you back," he said.

He made his way to the C-141 and, 30 minutes later, left Singapore.

CHAPTER 46

Carson was hospitalized for a week and cleared his name after several state departments and FBI officials explained away the house fire and his escape from a group of thieves. They had tried to kidnap the professional golfer and designer to use his influences in the community to enter Fort Canning to rob the gold amulets, rings, and diamonds.

The bullet passed through his leg and luckily did not fracture a bone. A military doctor ordered he would be on crutches for the next six weeks.

The Jordons were flown back on a C-17 to Wright Patterson AFB and made their way to Christ Hospital by limousine.

Elizabeth had called Estelle and made plans to meet her at the hospital. Elizabeth was excited to see Janet's family and share the experience of their first grandson. Estelle, Cynthia, Edwin, and Teresa met them in the nursery when they arrived. Elizabeth got a wheelchair for Carson and rolled him over to see Jeremy. They tapped on the window to get the attention of the nurse.

"Can we hold him for a few minutes, please?" Elizabeth said loudly. The nurse picked up Jeremy and walked out.

"I suppose you're the grandparents," she said.

"Yes, we are," Elizabeth and Teresa said in unison.

"Well, I am taking the baby to see Mama in recovery. If you will follow me, you can all share the bundle of Joy," the nurse said.

Elizabeth hugged Teresa. "Congratulations, Grandma," she said. "How is Janet?"

"Recovering. And all vitals are back to normal," Teresa said. "Wait, why aren't you in Georgia?"

"Georgia?" Elizabeth asked. "We don't move for another month. Why?"

"Jacob came out and told me he would meet the realtor who contacted you with some terrible news."

"What terrible news?" Carson interrupted.

"Something about an electrical fire," she said.

"Did Jacob say who the realtor was who called?" Elizabeth asked.

"Well, he was speaking to him on the phone, and I think Jacob thanked him. His name was Zack," Teresa said.

Both Elizabeth and Carson looked at each other, panicked.

"Auntie, we have to get to Georgia right away," Elizabeth said. "Do you have a car I can borrow?"

"I drove your aunt here from New York," Cynthia said. "Let's all go. I will drive."

Elizabeth wheeled Carson to the Chevy Blazer, and Estelle sat next to him in the back seat.

Elizabeth slammed her door shut. "Let's go, Cynthia!"

Cynthia peeled out of the hospital parking lot.

Elizabeth pulled out her new Nokia and received a voicemail. She pressed the button to hear the message.

"Elizabeth, your son is a delight. We have been talking for hours. I slapped him around a bit for mouthing off to an elder. I hope you don't mind. Bring me the disk, and you all can go home to celebrate the birth of your grandson. I'm waiting!"

Her next call was to the Georgia State Police.

"Sir, we think my son has been kidnapped at our new home in Macon."

"You think?" he said.

"Yes, we received a message that there was a fire, and our realtor would meet him for us. But the realtor is actually a criminal holding him hostage," she said.

"Wow. I think that story is going to be a bestseller, lady," the Georgia state officer replied and hung up.

"Uh! The nerve of that man!" Elizabeth said.

She made another call to a friend she had not spoken to in nearly a year.

"Is Ricardo around the bar?" she asked. "Tell him it's Liz, and I need help."

"How have you been, young lady?" Ricardo asked.

"I wish I had time to catch up, but I need your help."

"Tell me what you need. A property?" he asked.

"No, not really. I need some muscle," she replied.

Elizabeth explained what was happening at their new home in Macon, Georgia. Ricardo was an old friend of her father who played piano at his bars. Elizabeth was sure he was linked to the mafia, but he was like an adopted father after hers passed. He had rented them countless properties he owned before they were sent overseas.

"I will send a page with our address in Macon, Georgia," she said.

"Honey, I already have it," he laughed. "I will see you in a few hours."

The following six hours were nerve-wracking, and it gave both Jordons time to explain how there had been some confusion with recent events.

"No, Estelle, we are not working with the CIA," Carson laughed. "The FBI asked us to assist in helping with an overseas case involving a ring of thieves. They broke into our home searching for some drawings I had for the golf course at a resort displaying Singapore state jewelry valued at millions of dollars."

"Well, that makes more sense," Estelle said. "But who has kidnapped Jacob?"

"This could be a prank or someone angry about the incident in Singapore," he explained.

"We will call the local police when we arrive," Elizabeth said, facing her aunt.

The orange sun hid behind the clouds over the horizon. They passed the moss trees and a bright cherry sign which read, *Welcome to the home of wine.*

"Sure doesn't smell like wine, Cherie," Cynthia said.

There was a pungent odor seeping into the blazer.

"Smells like sulfur," explained Carson. "It's called the Macon Funk."

Cynthia laughed so hard that she almost ran off the road.

"Keep your eyes on the road, Cynthia," Elizabeth warned.

"Sorry," she said.

"No problem," Carson replied. "We are headed down the next street, which is College Hill Street.

Cynthia turned down the street, and Elizabeth stopped her at the fourth house.

"Please stay here with Estelle," Elizabeth asked.

Elizabeth nearly sprang from the Blazer. She grabbed Carson's crutches and headed to the front door.

"Elizabeth, this guy is crazy," he said. "I have the disk he needs, and we need to just give it to him and get Jacob out safely."

"We are going to be fine," she said.

They walked through the front door, and Zack was sitting on a fold-out chair, pointing a Colt at them.

"Mommy and Daddy came for you, Jacob," he said.

"Listen here, Zack or Chinese Leopard or whatever your real name is, we have the disk and want our son left out of this," Elizabeth said.

"Wow, now you're ready to cooperate. I thought you would give up the other piece after I shot your husband," he said. "Of course, you ruined my party."

"You murdered my friend!" she retorted.

"Okay, she deserved it," he said.

"Let our son go, and I will hand it over," she said.

"Sure, untie him, and he can leave," Zack said.

"But Mom," Jacob said.

"Son, leave the house like your mom asked," Carson said. Jacob walked out and saw his Aunt Estelle waving out a car window. He walked to the vehicle and got inside.

"Excuse me, both of you. I have to make a call," Cynthia said.

CHAPTER 47

"Okay, let's get this over with, Zack," Carson told the Chinese Leopard.

"Not quite yet," he said. "I will take the disk, but I will leave with Elizabeth in tow."

"What?" Elizabeth said, reaching into her purse for the disk. Her hand found the chapstick.

"We will be happy together, and I am going to be rich beyond belief, and I can give you anything you desire."

"How about the kiss you gave me while in Germany?"

"Yes. I want Carson to know I was your first and will be your last. So, hand me the disk, and I will kiss you to go along with it."

"Sure," she said, and Carson turned to face her. He had a furious and jealous look on his face. "This humid weather makes my lips dry. I am going to put on some lip balm."

"Go for it," Zack said.

Elizabeth opened one side of the chapstick and applied a layer on each lip. And then spread the other side and applied lip gloss.

"Ready?" she asked.

Zack walked over, snatched the fractured disk from her hand, and kissed her.

"How about that kiss, Carson?" he said confidently. "Okay, let's get out of here, Elizabeth."

"Not sure I want to do that, exactly. And you won't either."

Zack felt very strange, and his muscles ached terribly. His lips were turning blue, and his head's veins began to bulge.

"What did you do to me, bitch?" he asked as he tried to reach for his gun and fell to the ground. He foamed at the mouth and struggled to breathe.

"You should be careful who you kiss," she said.

"Good show, Elizabeth." The shadow stepped forward.

"Brad Wilson?" she questioned. "I haven't seen you for a while."

"Yeah, I guess so, huh?" he replied. "Well, things have changed. As you may know, I was one of the people left behind after a mission with four other case officers. I was shot, beaten, and tortured. Langley stopped looking for the throw-away, so I switched alliances. I work for the CCP, and I thank you for providing the disk."

Wilson picked up the Colt and pried the disk out of his partner's hand.

"You see, the disk has the last component of a toxic chemical which kills instantly. The final ingredient helps it spread from human to human. The disk also has names of all Chinese double agents," he said. "But the big payoff is the specs to build the W-88 ballistic missile which the Chinese intend to launch on the east coast of the U.S., spreading the toxin!"

"You wouldn't!" she said. "What happened to patriotism? Both you and Zack."

"Zack was a chump who I used. I set him up with the commandos. He must have gone batshit crazy living in the jungle. He believed he was the next coming of the mystical Chinese cat. Chinese Leopard?"

"Hold on. I saw you after the incident in Hong Kong. You were at the awards night and then heading on a mission," she retorted.

"Double agent. And after my team killed Matthews and you escaped, I knew you must have the disk."

"So, you sent your goons to our place to find it, but they weren't expecting me there," Carson said.

"Yes, unfortunately. Well, it has been nice chatting with you, but I must depart."

The front door slammed open, and several people yelled "freeze" as they pointed guns at Wilson.

"Cynthia?" Elizabeth said, looking at her friend from New Orleans, who was wearing a chain with a badge around her neck.

"FBI, drop the gun and down on your knees. Lace your fingers on top of your head," she said.

Another loud sound came from the back door, and Ricardo and his crew walked in. "Hey, sugar pie, you okay?" Ricardo asked.

"Now I'm good," she said.

Carson turned to his wife. "Did you know Nurse Cynthia was an FBI agent?"

"Hell no. I am as surprised as you," she said.

Several agents surrounded Wilson. They cuffed him and led him out of the house.

"Cynthia, where is Jacob and my aunt?" she asked.

"Cherie, they are in the Blazer and doing just fine," she said.

"You have so much explaining to do," Elizabeth said and hugged her.

"You do too, but not to me. I am sure the CIA will have a debriefing hearing, and testimony will be required about the top-secret disk that the FBI has now confiscated," she explained. "But Carson and your secret are safe with me."

"Thanks for taking care of us," she said. "And now you're part of the family. Got it?"

"Got it," she said. "Now, take my Chevy and get back to Cincinnati to enjoy your Grandson."

"Thanks, but I think we'll all fly back home." She laughed, and they hugged one more time.

Epilogue

J acob nearly ran into several nurses at Christ Hospital trying to get to his wife and newborn son. He felt alive after realizing a crazy maniac wanted to take the life of him and his parents. He was thankful to be with Janet and his son.

Janet had been through so much and was being released at the end of the day. The Jordons passed around Jeremy and took pictures. They ordered in dinner and celebrated their grandson's birth.

"Elizabeth, let's give Janet and Jacob a few moments alone, okay?" Carson asked. "Let's grab a cup of coffee."

"Sure, honey," she replied, and they headed down to a cafeteria that was still open and serving pecan pie.

"The disk the FBI has is a fake," he said. "I made up the story about there being two pieces and cut it precisely so they would fit together."

"Fake?" Elizabeth laughed and scowled. "And you're telling me this now?"

"I tossed the original in a lake filled with crocodiles at the Singapore Zoo," he explained. "I was being hunted, and I decided no one should have that information."

Elizabeth looked at her husband, leaned over the table, and kissed him softly on the lips.

His pager began to beep, and he grabbed it to read the message.

"Boy, this pecan pie is great with coffee," he said.

"Carson Jordon, I already know we are moving to Georgia."

"I wouldn't be so sure, Mrs. Jordon," he said.

"What was the message on your pager?"

"How do you like pistachio ice cream?" Carson asked.

"Pistachios? I am not following," Elizabeth said.

"Ankara, Turkey, babe. Did you know they are the third largest producer of pistachios?"

"Turkey, huh? That's nuts," she said.

Acknowledgments

By Kathryn Raaker

I want to thank God for the ability to co-author the second book of the series "Elizabeth Bromwell, the Case of The Chinese Leopard." I want to thank my new co-author, Robert Taggart, who inspired me to move forward with this novel in the series, and for writing and editing this book. We spent many hours on the phone, Skype, and sending emails back and forth to be able to generate this inspiring novel. I believe it will educate and entertain the readers and keep them on the edge of their seats. I also want to thank my dear husband, Bill Raaker, who supports everything that I do. I want to also thank my children Robert, Jeff and Jenny, and all my grandchildren, my daughters-in-law, for their love, support, and encouragement. And lastly, I want thank Janie Jessee and Jan-Carol Publishing for believing in our series and supporting us throughout the process of publishing our novel.

By Robert Taggart

I am blessed and thank my wife, Crystal, for her enthusiasm during many long nights of researching and writing. Thank you to my co-author, Kathryn Raaker, whose motherly love, dedication, and creativity helped me to share this adventure. I would like to acknowledge all of my children, family members, and friends for listening and passing on their ideas. Cheers to my long-time friend and personal editor, Michael Carroll, for his insights, and impactful editorial skills. Finally, thank you to Janie Jessee of Jan-Carol Publishing for keeping me focused and on task.

www.ingramcontent.com/pod-product-compliance
Lightning Source LLC
Chambersburg PA
CBHW050357030726
47503CB00006B/1891